HER DARK HEART

DARK SPELL SERIES BOOK 6

ISRA SRAVENHEART

CONTENTS

DEDICATION

To the real Astrid,
thank you for everything!
Even in the depths of despair, hatred and separation, you ignited the fire in
my heart! You made it burn with sheer passion and desire. Only you held
the power to make it glow, deeply penetrating it with such love and beauty.
An act that is impossible to forget.
Trust me, I will never forget it.

To the real Klinq...
We were friends once.
You taught me a lesson that I needed to grow, and needless to say, I have
done that because of that lesson!

To the real Everilda,
May you one day find peace in your heart.
May you also learn that others are not to be trampled upon.
I can only hope you learn this and break free from your pain and
desperation.

1

It was at dusk on a summer night as the pink skies darkened that a raven flew in from beneath the clouds and landed on a grassy bank in the middle of a great forest. At first glance, it was just a raven. Its beady black eyes held the tiniest hint of yellow and its black wings shimmered in the last rays of sun.

Then, a moment later, you would have realized this raven was not just any raven; his form shifted into that of a man. The man admired his handsome new appearance and muttered under his breath a few chosen words so quietly that they could not be heard by human ears, nor would he want them to be.

This raven was Astrid, the faithful lover of Lady Isra, a witch who dwelled in the forest.

A year ago, her tower disappeared from view. Astrid had insisted on this as a very important security measure; he was determined to keep the witch from human eyes and wanted to maximize her safety. But of course, she was more than capable of looking after herself, being a witch and all.

He and Lady Isra had been together for about a year and a half now and were close companions. He loved the witch's dark heart and was very fond of her, as she was of him. Any time he went out, he would transform himself back into his raven form.

The reason he was so careful when he ventured in and out was that Lady Isra and Astrid's tower had been cloaked from all human eyes with a powerful invisibility spell, and only a few specially chosen words made it visible. It worked the same way as a door; only he and Lady Isra had the metaphysical key that opened the dark fortress that was their home.

A few things had changed in the tower since Astrid had been with Lady Isra. The interior had been modified slightly. He preferred the scarlet red that now dominated most of the building, creating a vibrant energy. Their bedroom was a mix of purple, red, and black with a black bed, bedspread, and curtains showcased by purple and black walls. All of this was done as if by magic.

Astrid had become an expert at transforming since Lady Isra had shifted him into human form. Still, he never saw himself as a human, as this form was just a body. He had learned how to work and manage his energy better and could aid Lady Isra on a number of her spells. She had taught him much and he was a fast learner; he didn't need a single tool to work his magic.

Not just any raven could do these things that Astrid was doing. Lady Isra was proud of how accomplished he had become. Astrid had mastered shape-shifting well and although he struggled with reading human books, he had completed the study quickly and learned more every day.

But what about Lady Isra? What about her powers, you might wonder? Had they grown or had they weakened?

Well, neither had happened. Since her revenge on Kane, she found she didn't need to use magic. But this contentment was also due to Astrid's presence. She had found her other half; she was complete now. Still dark, but she didn't need to use magic.

But before you ask, no; she had *not* turned over a new leaf.

When you are dark, you are dark. You don't go back. Lady Isra had no intention of going back either; she wasn't about to become

Miss Goody Two-Shoes who would go dancing off into the light. No, that would be rather boring, wouldn't it?

After totally destroying Kane, she found she didn't really have a need for magic. The impulses and the power it gave her were still there, but she didn't need it. As to whether you would consider that good or bad? Well, I will allow you to make your own judgments.

Lady Isra was quite happy with it all. She looked radiant with her long, black, curly hair that hung down to her bottom. Her piercing green eyes looked even greener, as if brightened with lightning.

But what else has been happening around the place, you ask?

Astrid and Lady Isra were as strong as they could ever be in their union, filled with power, love, and trust. Their loyalty was as solid as the walls of the tower themselves. Nothing could ever break it or tear it down; it was *that* mighty and powerful of a force to be reckoned with and it seemed nothing could destroy or interfere with the energy and power between them.

After Kane's demise, it was Astrid who'd suggested the tower be cloaked from the human world so Lady Isra could be protected. It was not clear why he had wanted this, but her location and the fact that she was still around was to remain a closely guarded secret. It was all his doing; he had insisted. Lady Isra had no part in it except that she'd agreed to his request as she was pleased by how much he cared about her safety and well-being.

Despite knowing that she could protect herself, she had agreed to his request and the tower was cast under a powerful invisibility spell. Nobody except Astrid and Lady Isra would have any clue over its existence; humans would not be able to find it, and magical folk would have an equally hard job as it was so well hidden. Anybody who tried would, in fact, be stupid to do so.

Astrid paused for a moment as he felt an energy go through him and then stepped inside. It was quiet, but he called for Lady Isra to see if she was home. He was very cautious about her going out, but she was too much of a free spirit and often left for lonely walks. Fear pricked his heart as he called for her again.

Instantly she was there, letting him place a kiss on her forehead. It was a simple sign of protection and devotion, but it was something Lady Isra had not experienced for a very long time before she met Astrid.

"Good morning, love! I trust all is well in that ghastly human world?" she joked as he placed his hands gently around her neck and pulled her into an embrace.

"Yes, they are fine," he mumbled into her hair, "but still so terribly human."

She chuckled and then paused as she heard sounds coming from outside. Astrid heard it too and he saw her eyes dart to the window.

"What was that, Astrid?"

"I have no idea, but I hope for their sake that they know who I am."

She thought to herself, *Well, they may not, but I know who you are.*

He went to the window to see what it was. Now of course with the tower being cloaked, anyone looking up toward the tower would have only seen the sky. That's how strong the cloaking of the invisibility spell was—not that Astrid was sure that they even needed it. For who would dare enter the home of a witch?

Whoever was out there making that racket clearly had a death wish.

Suddenly, and much to the surprise of Lady Isra, Astrid dashed downstairs and out the door, as if his heart were on fire.

2

Astrid was fast and could quickly be heard shouting at someone. Lady Isra surveyed the scene carefully as she looked out of the window. Then Astrid rushed back in, cursing and shouting.

He approached the stairs of the tower and brought the thing he had been dragging along with him. Upon closer inspection, Lady Isra could see it was a gnome. A short but terrified gnome. He didn't have any standards of cleanliness or sense of style; his clothes were worn and tattered, and his hair was peeking out from under his hat.

Astrid had him held by the ear and he was clearly suffering, which Lady Isra seemed to find amusing; she laughed when she saw the gnome whimpering in fear and grimacing in pain. Astrid looked at the witch and then turned to look directly at the gnome.

"I found this parasite lurking around outside! He could see us as well as the tower and so he is somehow able to get through the invisibility spell we put on it."

"Hmm, he *is* a gnome. He has magic in him. But *what* was he doing snooping around outside?" Lady Isra inquired harshly.

Astrid looked at the gnome again and boomed, "Good question, so what *were* you doing outside?"

The gnome—who was already whimpering and very shaken at having his ear tugged so roughly by the raven-man—began to speak.

"I beg you, please spare me. I mean you no harm, I was just looking for a safe place in the woods as I cannot go back home. I will be killed if I do!" He wailed and whined a little as he finished.

The gnome's story wasn't convincing, and Lady Isra wasn't about to be moved by a common sob story, but she decided to play along and looked to Astrid cheerfully.

"Well, I suppose he could be useful around here every now and then when the moment strikes," she joked as she waited for his response.

"Useful is a term that should be used very lightly," Astrid remarked.

The witch sniggered. She loved his little sarcastic remarks.

"Hmm, what can you do, my fine fellow, and please do tell me your name?" she asked and tapped her foot impatiently while she waited for him to answer her questions.

Astrid loosened his grip on him and he straightened himself and replied, "My name is Klinq. I am from a village a little journey from here named Spindlevitch."

Lady Isra immediately began to shriek in fits of laughter. Astrid looked puzzled; he did not know why the witch was laughing. Spindlevitch—she knew the name, and that wasn't the only reason she was laughing. She fondly remembered that it was the home village of Lillian, the maiden she had brutally killed a year ago to spite Kane.

"Spindlevitch. What a beautiful place! I love it there!" she announced wickedly.

Astrid, who was still very puzzled at the way she was acting, did not recognize the name of the place, and he did not know why Lady Isra found it so amusing.

"You know of it?" Klinq asked the witch inquiringly.

Lady Isra laughed as she looked at the gnome and sharply replied with a hint of evil in her voice. "Yes, I know it *very* well, a nice place to visit, especially if you are human."

Klinq looked puzzled as to why she was acting so oddly.

"Well, it is settled then, Klinq. Welcome to your new home and in return for my kind hospitality, I will require you to be my eyes and ears to the human world," she instructed as he noted her words carefully.

He had just been employed as a spy for a witch. How exciting ... or maybe not. He had to admit he was still frightened and had no idea who she was or what she was capable of, but it was too late to chicken out now. He felt that rejecting her offer might offend her, and he did not want to be one to offend a witch. It was the way she manically laughed that scared him the most.

Klinq didn't have a very good track record for making anything good. He did have a well-known reputation for messing things up though, and this was something he should have thought about before accepting Lady Isra's offer. Was she being genuinely nice, or was there something more menacing behind it?

Yes, she wanted a spy for the human world. Yes, she could not stand the humans to the point their very existence made her want to vomit. Any act of kindness or good repulsed her unless it was from Astrid, so it begged the question why she had offered this desperate gnome a home and more importantly, a job. Not a good one, but a job nonetheless.

Klinq was shown his quarters that oddly enough were the same basement the slave boy, Kane, was once held hostage in, but now it was rather different in appearance. The chains had been tidied away, hoisted on a side wall and the dark, dreary walls had been painted a neutral earth color, more appropriate for a dark hole. And although the room was fairly small, it looked much bigger in perspective, like it could have a much more useful purpose.

Astrid turned to leave after showing Klinq everything, and it was then that Klinq noticed there was a large, heavy padlock hung upon a nail on the wall and the keys to it were not there; this room was being kept this way for a reason.

Klinq settled his rucksack on the antique bed and emptied his things. He took a glance at his new home; a nice place despite its weird but yet mysterious inhabitants. He didn't pay too much attention to Lady Isra or Astrid. As far as he could gather, they were a couple, very close with one another and she was a witch.

He also didn't know too much about what his new role would entail, just that he would be a spy. He was informed that Lady Isra would give instructions on his role and what she wanted him to do shortly, so there was nothing more he could do for now but pass the night. He placed his things on the bed which he was now eyeing up happily as he listened to the wind outside howl.

KLINQ WOKE up the next morning very early to prepare himself. He didn't want to mess up—he was known for messing up—but he figured if he planned it strategically in his head before being instructed that everything would be okay.

He didn't know what he would be asked to do. He knew his new employer was a witch and not a very nice one at that. His first impressions of her weren't good, but he hoped that she would be nice to him and consider his good qualities, even though those were very few.

He brushed his scruffy brown hair as best as he could and made his way upstairs where there was loud morning laughter. He got closer and recognized the voices as Lady Isra and Astrid. They had been laughing over something that must have been so amusingly funny that both their faces were red as apples. Astrid had his arms wrapped around the witch's waist while she shrieked with laughter as they lay on the couch.

Klinq approached slowly. As he opened the door, they both straightened themselves up immediately but were still very close together. Lady Isra was the one to greet Klinq formally while Astrid stared at the gnome; this made him self-conscious, as he could feel that his bald patch on the top of his head was showing.

"So, I presume you passed the night in my basement well?" she inquired.

Klinq looked rather amused at this and asked, "Basement?"

"Yes. Before you came here, it was used to hold my slave boy. There have been a few changes here since then," she added, and noticed Klinq was quite nervous.

Lady Isra gave him a folded piece of parchment, and she watched the gnome's face as he read it.

3

He folded the piece of parchment and put it in his pocket. He had now been given his orders and left the tower at once as he had been informed of what he needed to do. He wandered nervously into the forest and set off about his task. The witch had given him clear instructions: be her eyes and ears to the human world. She had also given him a stern warning.

Betray me and I will kill you.

The last part was what had stuck in his head the most.

So, with the witch's words lingering in his mind, Klinq started on his long journey through the forest and to—in Lady Isra's words—the human world.

Quietly, he started to walk through the dark forest, taking the time and care to notice every single tree he walked past as he steadied ahead on his journey. He did not know what he would be looking for or what he would find, but he knew he had to keep his eyes open as that was also one of Lady Isra's detailed instructions. He was nervous and scared and didn't quite know what he had gotten himself into.

He knew Lady Isra would not be kind to him if he failed; she had already revealed to him that she'd once held a slave in the basement which was now Klinq's home. He needed to be extra careful with his new job and do his best to not mess anything up. He hoped that he could do this. He *hoped*.

He walked for a while until he saw the sight of some people praying and dancing together in front of a fire in the forest. They seemed like an unusual group which caught his attention, so he hid behind an oak tree to get a closer look at what was occurring.

He watched as the women and men gathered around the fire, dancing and singing with happy, smiling faces that were proud to be at such a joyous occasion. It was clear the group of happy folk was spiritual practitioners of some kind, but it wasn't clear just what they were. Since they were dancing in front of a fire, he surmised it would be accurate to say this was a gathering of the spiritual nature.

There was one woman in particular who had caught his attention.

She was young and had purple hair that went down to her shoulders. He watched as she danced and swayed with her fellow chanters. She had something about her, something in her spirit that caught Klinq's eye. She didn't notice that she was being watched; she was so focused on her task.

Klinq—not knowing much about it himself—found it rather enchanting, but he feared he was about to be discovered as he suddenly felt the need to sneeze. And sneezed he did, very loudly which startled the group and they stopped what they were doing. The young woman shifted her focus to the tree, exactly where Klinq had hidden himself, and made her way over to it.

She placed her hand on the tree's trunk and whispered, "Oh, great spirit inside this tree, thou shall now reveal thyself to me!"

She waited a moment to see if anything would arise from the tree, but nothing came much to her disappointment as she was curious to know what creature had made the noise that had disrupted the ritual.

She called out to one of her fellow women and announced softly, "I do not know what it was, perhaps it was a nature spirit of some kind and we caught its wild curiosity, but it seems to have vanished now."

Klinq, who was very worried about being discovered, was desperately thinking of a way out of his situation. How would he get away without being seen? He knew magic but not a lot, and any spells he tried to do normally backfired on him, so this would not be an easy feat to conquer.

He closed his eyes and began to think hard, hoping and praying that the young woman would not see him, as he did not want to be discovered. After all, he was on a secret spy mission for a rather evil witch, and he could quite easily guarantee that Lady Isra would not engage in spiritual acts with others in such a loving way as this woman had.

He had two choices: either be discovered by the young woman and be asked what he was doing watching her people or get back to Lady Isra without being seen and risk incurring her wrath at how stupid he had been.

Not good choices—both of them had a downside—but he had to choose one of them and fast. However, it seemed now that his choice had been made for him; the young woman was making her way over to him. He had been seen!

He squirmed as she approached, but she spoke softly. "Do not be afraid, for I will not harm you. Why are you hiding behind this magnificent oak tree?" she inquired.

Klinq looked as if he wanted to run away from her as swiftly as possible. He straightened himself as best as he could in his response to her and bravely replied.

"I am in hiding because I thought I saw something, and I got frightened. I thought if I stayed behind here long enough, the thing that frightened me would surely go away!"

She seemed to believe his wild story.

The young woman held his hand and smiled. "Well, there is nothing here to harm you now. My name is Contessia, and I live here in the woods with my clan. What's your name?" she asked sweetly.

Klinq gazed into young Contessia's eyes and looked fondly upon her for giving him such kindness before he answered.

"I am Klinq, and I work for a witch, Lady Isra, who lives nearby from here; in fact, I must go soon as she will be wondering where I am."

He quickly realized he had made a mistake. And a *very* big mistake at that. He had been strictly told to keep Lady Isra a secret from the human world and he had now failed at that by revealing her identity *and* what she was to the young woman. He had not only revealed that Lady Isra was a witch, but also that he was working for her. She would not be best pleased with him.

Oh shit, what a useless, dumb idiot I am! he thought to himself before realizing he was still in the presence of Contessia.

Contessia looked at the gnome and smiled while replying, "I hope our paths cross once more, Sir Klinq."

Klinq began fumbling around in his bag and was ready to make his way back to Lady Isra. He tried to make eye contact with Contessia as he proceeded to say goodbye to his newfound friend.

"Well, it has been a most wondrous occasion meeting you, but I must get back to the witch, for if I am late and she will most surely scold me."

Contessia put her hand on his shoulder. "I am a witch too, but I am good. My clan and I practice love and caring as well as the balance and beauty of nature," she announced proudly.

A good witch? Is there such a thing? he thought.

Klinq realized he didn't know that much about witches or what they practiced. He decided he rather liked witches, and this new stranger in the woods had given him a whole new interest in the subject.

He had only known bad witches; he had never even heard of a good witch. If he was being honest, he tried not to know much about bad witches, but Klinq, being what he was (stupid and clumsy), often found witches to be his most favorable employers.

Again, he pondered the idea of a good witch. Something like that could only be believed in fairy tales. That was his belief.

Klinq admired the young Contessia in the moment and broke into a small smile while saying, "I am sure what you do is nothing but beautiful. I must go. Goodbye."

Contessia continued. "If you need help or advice or someone to come to, you know where to find us. I don't believe someone should be surrounded by dark forces; it is not the true magic way."

Contessia believed in the good and only the good. She was true to her beliefs, and she believed that Klinq should not have been working for Lady Isra, who in Contessia's eyes, was a very bad witch and not doing true magic.

Oh god, I hope these two ladies never meet face to face, he thought as he remembered Contessia's final words and headed back into the forest to make his way to the tower.

Klinq practically marched to get back to Lady Isra's tower; he wanted to arrive again as soon as he could, for he had to think of what to say to her. The reason? Lady Isra had sent Klinq on a mission as her spy for the human world. A mission to see what he could discover and find out about the humans as she had been curious.

He had failed her greatly by not only revealing to Contessia that Lady Isra was a witch and that she was a wicked one at that, but he had also let slip to Contessia that he was working for Lady Isra. Not a wise move at all, no; he had been told to keep things a secret, especially her identity.

He was not looking forward to getting back there but knew he had to nonetheless, and quickly. He hoped he could keep his mess-up a secret. And so he reflected on this and thought about how badly he had messed up, and this was not just one mess up—it had been more than one thing he had revealed.

Contessia had kindly told Klinq if he needed someone, she would be there for him, which gave him the idea that they might meet again. But two failures in one day, could it get any worse for him? Was there anything else he would screw up?

It was best if he did not give it too much thought. He was worrying himself sick!

He was more concerned about what would happen when he was found out rather than what his new friend thought. She had voiced her views over it already because she had said that dark magic was not a true form of magic. Klinq strongly doubted that Lady Isra would agree with that viewpoint.

4

Carefully and quietly, he opened the huge tower door after uttering the specially chosen set of words that kept it hidden from the human world and breathed deeply as he prepared to be greeted by his employers.

He knew he ought to tread carefully and watch each and every step and move he made while living with these beings, namely the witch, for if he fucked up she would surely do something nasty to him, and he did not want that. She would know if he had fucked up too, and that was what had worried him the most.

He gathered his thoughts as he approached the staircase, but he was distracted by sounds of joy coming from the floor above. Sounds of joy and happiness in *this* establishment?

He couldn't believe his ears. Surely there could be no joy in such a place of hatred and evil! He was very wrong with that statement, because today there was joy and happiness in the tower of the dark one and her beloved.

Klinq slowly climbed the staircase, listening as he reached the top. He decided to lurk in the doorway, paying attention to what was happening in the other room.

Astrid had given Lady Isra a box lovingly wrapped with ribbon. There was no clue as to what it was inside, but he presented it to her with a kiss.

Klinq paid great attention as he watched the witch open the box and to his surprise as well as Lady Isra's, there was a small black kitten inside which had also had a ribbon around its neck. She cradled the kitten proudly and smiled back at her lover as she held it in her arms.

"What a beautiful baby!" she announced, proudly stroking the kitten's head.

The raven-man Astrid replied softly, "I got him for you so you'd have a companion when I am not here."

Astrid was in love with the witch—this was no secret—and today, he had shown his affection to her by presenting her with a gift. He watched with wide eyes as his lover, the dark witch he had grown to know and love, sweetly held her tiny kitten in such a way that he could not help but admire. His heart melted at her very presence. He stammered in his thoughts as he watched this being softly attending to the new arrival in the household with such care and love.

Hard to believe such affection could come from a dark soul such as Lady Isra ... however, what he saw right then from his lover was real. He saw the purity of her heart.

She smiled at Astrid and declared proudly, "I will name this little one Onyx, as he is jet black and a real, beautiful dark soul."

The kitten, less than a few weeks old, looked tired and sleepy in the witch's arms. It closed its tiny eyes while she was holding him. Astrid got up to his feet and held little Onyx with her and looked at him fondly and gushed happily.

"Welcome, little Onyx, to the dark household!" He stroked his ears gently and touched Lady Isra's shoulder and whispered, "He will be sleepy soon. We should find a place for him to rest. He has had a very exciting day."

She agreed and carefully carried the little kitten to a window seat and placed him comfortably on top of a shawl. "Sleep well, my precious dark one," she cooed as she left him to get much-needed rest.

Klinq was still listening in the doorway, but now he entered the room.

Lady Isra saw his entrance and remarked, "Well, it seems this one is back from their travels. Please, do tell me, what did you find on your little trip?" she questioned sweetly but with a hint of sarcasm in her voice.

Her sarcastic remarks could always bring even the strongest person into a trembling mess within a nanosecond. Klinq wasn't a trembling mess yet, but she did intimidate him quite a lot. He looked at her with much sincerity and he noted her sarcasm.

"Yes, I saw something very interesting. It intrigued me. I found a coven in the woods. I even made friends."

She laughed at the dim-witted gnome and remarked to Astrid, "Oh my, our little Klinq went into the woods and made some friends. What an eventful day this has been!"

Astrid laughed but said nothing. He let Lady Isra be in control with the gnome and left her to her tirade. She continued, adding questions to her mocking of him. "A coven, hmm? I have heard of those. What kind?" she asked.

Klinq hastily fiddled with his clothing. He was nervous. She *made* him nervous. He didn't want to tell her what he was about to tell her, although he knew if he didn't, she would metaphorically have him on a plate. He began anxiously, and Isra's eyes moved all over him as she sensed his anxiety.

"They were good witches with love and compassion. I do not know much about witches or what they do so I found them to be very intriguing," he admitted.

She watched his body language closely. Lady Isra laughed menacingly; she found this highly amusing. *Of course, you do not know about witches, you are dumb and stupid and it's a wonder any of them employ you as there is virtually no good use for you anywhere,* she thought to herself.

She commented to him, "It sounds like you met the love and light brigade. They preach about peace, love, and goodness. Oh, how it makes me want to vomit!"

She was reminded of her own experience in that world. She hated the way they preached about their "do good and be good" role. She hated being controlled by a set of rules that did not fit her standards. She hated the way that no matter how much love she had shown, she got none back in return for her efforts. It was a false and self-conceited world and she hated it with a passion. The love and light thing was now long past her, but she still hated the memory of it.

Isra suddenly controlled her fast-moving thoughts and turned her attention back to Klinq, who was reciting his very own passion.

He began to waffle as he said, "They seemed like a nice bunch of ordinary folk who just want to love the world and bring happiness to all they meet. I don't understand why you would have such hatred for something so beautiful as love."

The witch glared at him. Astrid watched as she did this; he watched her eyes all over Klinq in that moment. He knew she was dark and he knew she wasn't fond of love, but he didn't realize just how much the light side angered her. He could see her about to blow up inside as he watched her talk about it. He had to admit he didn't know too much about her past but he knew that right now, Klinq's shoes were not a good place to be in. He stayed observant and kept quiet.

Klinq's waffling did not impress Lady Isra. "That loving attitude that they preach is all well and good but when it comes to the love they *give*, it is nonexistent and false."

Klinq whispered, "I am sorry. I did not know that; they seemed okay to me."

Lady Isra fixed her eyes on the gnome sharply and then looked away again as she sighed.

"Unfortunately, Klinq, I have seen both sides. They are very loving when it comes to the preaching that they care about every human and every animal in this world, but the second someone has something real and they need—and I mean *really* need—love and understanding, those so-called love and light beings are nowhere to be found. They abandon and disregard you like yesterday's trash. Trust me, I know."

She looked out of the window and surveyed the empty forest that surrounded her home.

5

———————

It was quiet today, not a single animal in sight.

She turned back to Klinq and announced, "I think that is enough for you today. You have done good work. I apologize for my shortness but the love and light world is not something I have much fondness for."

Astrid, who had been watching the entire conversation between them, was quietly thinking about what had happened in her past to make her feel this way. He was thinking deeply about it, trying to understand the woman he loved. The woman who was so bitter about her past and hated anything that was loving or good. He knew she loved him, that was for certain, but he didn't understand why she had become this way.

Although Astrid himself was very dark in his mindset, he had a balance which separated the light and the dark. It kept him in good spirits and it gave him a wider outlook on life. Lady Isra was not balanced; she preferred the dark and the solitude. She lived there, and it was clear to Astrid that she did not want to change her ways.

She was dark as she was evil and she was happy with it. He could see now that something traumatic and real had made her this way and he was only just beginning to understand what that was.

Klinq nodded and replied, "Thank you, I will leave you in peace," and left the room to go back to the basement after being excused by the witch.

Astrid, still watching his beloved intensely, came up from behind her and asked softly, "What is it about them that makes you hurt so much?"

His loving touch warmed her, and it made her feel safe. She had never felt this with anyone else in her life before.

She smiled at his tight hold on her body and explained slowly, "It is something I never talk about for a good reason. It is not a place I want to be in ever again. Just the thought of it makes me shudder so I do what I do because that is the way it is. There is no love or good here in me."

He embraced her even tighter as he whispered in her ear, "I do not believe that to be true, as I see love in you. It is just shut away behind a great big wall that you have put up and built around yourself."

She tensed, but he continued softly. "I understand why you hate that world and I'm sorry I was not there to protect you from the falseness you felt from it, but I am here now, and I never want you to feel like that again."

She hastily moved from his embrace and pulled away. Isra wanted quiet time. It wasn't that she didn't want him to know about her past and it wasn't that she was pushing him away. She knew he had good intentions and was affectionate toward her, but she also needed her space, and this was why she was being distant with him.

A small, sweet kiss placed on his lips as she turned to leave the room let him know that his efforts were appreciated and that she was thankful to have him. It also let him know that she understood that he wanted to help but she just wasn't ready.

His eyes followed her carefully as she wandered out of their home and into the wilderness, the forest outside. He understood she needed time to be with herself but he did want to be there for her. However, she was not allowing him to do that.

She wandered far and wide into the forest and sat down on the grassy bank. She was quieting her mind as she sensed something, something calling to her. It wasn't Astrid; although she loved him and she knew she loved him, it wasn't him. She didn't want to hurt his feelings, so she had gone out to calm her restless mind and soothe herself with the wells of nature, something she did often to soothe herself down.

Astrid seemed a little shocked at her reaction but he understood why. She was a quiet, isolated spirit and sometimes all she really needed was herself to get by.

She focused on the magic that was calling to her. She continued to hear its call. It was strong and powerful. The energy floated around her in waves; she felt it. It was doing its very best at pulling her forward.

She was good at resisting however, and closed her eyes for a moment as she zeroed in on the energies fluttering around her aura and she caught it right there in its tracks. She put her hand out in front of her and with malevolent force, she shouted loudly, "NO! Go from where you came. You are not needed here."

Isra wasn't best impressed with any uninvited being or human contacting her, never mind some unknown magical energy that wanted her attention. She had been off balance today and a little upset, but stupid? Never. Whoever had been responsible for this energy that was trying to captivate Lady Isra had clearly underestimated her powers. She blasted it away within a fraction of a second.

She continued on her solitude before deciding that she would head home to Astrid. She decided she needed to talk to him. Some things he may not understand, but she was willing to confide in him about them.

Isra started her journey home by walking through the trees, appreciating the cool breeze that the wind had to offer as she felt it touch her skin. She was almost home when she noticed something standing directly in front of her tower in the distance. Now she had cloaked it very well under Astrid's request so this occurrence really baffled her.

Yes, a mortal (the slave boy, Kane) had been able to see her home once before, but that was before the cloaking. This was different. She walked closer to see what it was, making herself very clear to whoever it may be.

She laughed as the subject became visible to her. It was a young girl. She couldn't have been any older than nineteen and she had purple hair going down to her shoulders with blue eyes that peeked out from under her hair.

Lady Isra didn't recognize this individual that was looking around the grounds of her home, but she had taken an interest in her for whatever reason she was here, lurking around the home of a witch.

It wasn't clear who she was or what she was doing, but maybe she should have noted that her actions were being recorded by the eyes of a witch, and a particularly nasty one at that. However, she had no idea and was totally unaware that her spying had been observed.

The witch approached the girl and tapped her sharply on the shoulder. "Now just what may I ask, are you doing here?" she asked ferociously.

The young girl trembled and looked apologetic.

"Oh, I apologize! I was looking for a friend of mine I met yesterday in the woods. His name is Sir Klinq. He told me he worked for a witch and this is the only dark place in the whole forest so I was hoping I had the right place."

She had the right place all right, but whether it was the right place at the right time for *her* would be another story entirely!

Lady Isra studied the girl; she was human, but there was something about her. Something that she didn't normally see in humans. Something that had a bit of substance and an edge.

The girl that stood in front of the witch was poised in her appearance; she had a long white dress that flowed down to her ankles which only lengthened her small, slim frame. Her eyes met Isra's glaring pair sympathetically, despite being fearful of the witch.

Isra studied the girl again and replied, "You have the right place, child, and Sir Klinq as you so fondly called him is in his quarters resting right now. I'd be happy to take you to him however, I would like to know who I am speaking to. So, who are *you*?"

She smelt magic. It was real and strong. She could smell it from a mile away. It had a foul human odor that she vaguely remembered as the smell of fear.

The girl smiled and introduced herself. "Oh, I am Contessia, and my clan and I live in the forest. We practice love and beauty to all we meet."

Lady Isra quietly sniggered at the comment and led the girl toward the tower.

Thoughtfully she said, "You will have to be careful. This place doesn't often get viewed by humans on the inside and so anything that you see here, stays in here. Are my words understood?" she asked forcefully.

Contessia quietly nodded in agreement and off they went inside the tower. She was shocked; here she was, entering the witch's home It wasn't what she had expected at all. She expected it to be some old, rotting hole but instead it was more like a palace with solid walls and bold colors. Not the kind of place you would expect for a witch!

Lady Isra turned to Contessia and a raven landed on her shoulder.

"Oh yes, this is Astrid, he lives here too, but he is not all he seems," she said with a hint of mystery in her voice.

Contessia looked perturbed at the raven but said nothing. The whole place was giving her an eerie vibe and she just wanted to speak to Klinq, so in this instance, she kept her mouth shut.

Lady Isra started to lead her down to the basement, but then she stopped and said, "Let me speak with him for a moment, and then I will bring him to you."

Contessia nodded as she didn't want to argue. She watched as Lady Isra went down the steps.

6

own she went, disappearing swiftly to the bottom of the stairs. She knocked on the door loudly, pounding her fist against the wooden door. Klinq—upon hearing the loud knock—got to his feet and opened the door. He was curious as to why she was there.

"Oh, hello. I wasn't expecting you," he answered sheepishly.

The witch gave him a sly smile and responded, "No, neither was I." She hastened in her sarcasm and lowered her voice. "It seems you didn't tell me about your little friend on your travels in the forest yesterday. She is upstairs right now, but I believe her to be a troublemaker."

She stated this assertively as she looked at the gnome and studied the fear in his eyes.

Klinq looked down at the floor as he said, "Oh? She seems very nice to me."

Lady Isra stopped him in his tracks. "Yes, that is an observation you would make. Me, on the other hand, I question everything in my path."

She went back into her thoughts to recap on the events of the afternoon when she had experienced the weird energy in the forest

25

and meeting Contessia on the way home. She thought it was suspicious and that it was possible the two events were indeed linked. She thought about it again and paused.

H*mmm,* she pondered to herself, *I got a strange energy following me and when I got here, his little witch friend was outside my home.*

She continued. "I was almost attacked today while out; an energy tried to get me to go to it. I resisted. Not many can, but I did. Also, that doesn't mean whoever it was won't try again!"

They better not try anything like that again if they know what's good for them, she thought.

Lady Isra looked at Klinq and signaled for him to follow her. She opened the door and turned to leave before looking at him.

"I will be watching you and this girl very closely, Klinq, and believe me, if one tiny little thing seems wrong, I will act upon it and you and your little friend will live to regret it because I don't take kindly to betrayal." She finished sharply before adding, "You may go and talk to your friend now, but remember my words as you engage in conversation with this human."

Lady Isra and Klinq went up the steps; the walk to the hallway seemed extremely long. She was slow and her dress dragged on the floor as she climbed the staircase. Her words to him had been firm.

He felt that Contessia wasn't a problem, but Lady Isra was seeing her as one and that would prove to be a problem for him.

They entered the hallway and Lady Isra took control of the situation by taking Contessia by the arm and smiling sweetly as she announced, "I think it is time for a nice hot cup of tea," to which Contessia did not know where to look. She didn't seem comfortable with her arm linked in Lady Isra's, but she had no choice. The witch was in charge now.

"Klinq, make some chamomile tea," she instructed carefully.

Klinq's body language showed that he didn't know what was occurring and that he was just being loyal, doing his duties and keeping quiet. Being asked to make tea wasn't one of his duties, but he did as he was asked without uttering a word.

Klinq placed the tea on the window seat and went to the other side of the room to let the ladies talk. He didn't want to get in the way of anything. Lady Isra inspected the tea carefully and took a sip from the one she held in her hands. It was warm and the mint refreshed her as she breathed in its cool flavor.

Contessia hastily accepted her tea, although she didn't want it if she was honest. Nor did she want to be in this situation. She felt constricted, like her choices had been stolen from her. The witch was happy and relishing the moment as she sat next to Contessia who was saying nothing and sipping her tea slowly, abstaining from making any eye contact with Isra. Isra stared at the girl with much fascination and intrigue.

Isra gushed and said, "Well, what a lovely occasion this is. The sun is shining. It is just us ladies relaxing and enjoying a nice hot cup of tea."

Contessia replied, "Sure it is. This is not what I expected though." She sipped her tea and narrowed her eyes at the witch.

Isra was curious as to why she had said this, so she asked, "What were you expecting to happen after your delightful meeting with Klinq?"

Contessia was silent for a few moments before she answered. "This wasn't what I was envisioning when I was doing my ritual in the woods with my clan."

Lady Isra smiled and teased, "You do that Wiccan stuff, so this place and I must be like some dystopian fantasyland for you, child."

Contessia mildly laughed at the remark as she said firmly, "I try to stay away from anything that is covered in dark forces. It is a strong belief in my clan that being dark is bad."

Contessia was feeling nervous and didn't want to be in the presence of Lady Isra. If she could, she would have run out of there like a shot. She hated anything dark as it scared her. She feared it and what it could do if someone got close enough to unleash that kind of power. Lady Isra had that kind of power, therefore Isra made Contessia very nervous.

Lady Isra laughed, "Nonsense child, darkness is all around you.

You need to take a good look at yourself!" She glared at Contessia who was not laughing.

Take a good look at myself? she thought silently. *What is that supposed to mean? I am good and I do good,* she affirmed. *I will not let myself be covered in dark forces of malice and hatred that govern evil.*

She let these thoughts sink deep inside her soul and pondered them silently in her mind. Then she remembered she was still in the company of Lady Isra, but it had seemed like a daydream.

"I do look at myself and I don't see anything like that," she explained shortly while taking deep breaths.

The witch was beginning to really get on her nerves and she was feeling suffocated.

Lady Isra took the young girl's hand and smiled. "Darkness is in you; do not be afraid of it because that is when it will take you. Believe me, I know," she announced with a sly smile.

She paused and looked toward the door fondly with a smile. She was wondering where Astrid was; he didn't want to be in the way of this meeting between Contessia and Isra so he had transformed back into his raven form and was lurking around nearby, keeping well out of sight.

She was missing him though, and even though Contessia was sitting on her couch in her presence, the witch thought there would be no danger in leaving her charge unattended for a few minutes while she went and sought out her man.

She purred sweetly, "I have to go find the man of the house. I am sure you will be well while I am gone. It will only be for a few minutes."

Contessia—who was relieved to be away from the witch for a little while—mumbled, "Okay, that is fine with me," as Lady Isra smiled again and disappeared.

Contessia observed the room quietly and felt happy at being free of the witch's dominant nature for a little while. She noticed Klinq was no longer in the room; she hadn't even seen him leave. Klinq had gone back down to his basement. He was staying out of the way. He didn't want to interfere, so off he quietly went down to his dark hole like the coward he was.

He felt bad for not standing up for Contessia but unfortunately for her, he was weak. He couldn't stand up for himself so the chances of him doing it for someone else would be highly unlikely. Isra had gone upstairs and was headed to the bedroom on her search for Astrid. She stood in the doorway of the bedroom, scanning everything in the room as she looked for signs of his whereabouts. It was quiet and the window was open. It was normally closed.

She spotted him at last. Astrid was lying down on the bed. She couldn't tell if he was asleep but she climbed onto the bed and slowly maneuvered herself next to him which made him jerk awake and he impulsively wrapped his arms around her.

He whispered, "There you are. I was wondering when you would come up here and find me."

"I had company; there is a girl downstairs. I was entertaining," she said as he playfully kissed her neck and held her close to him as she lay in his arms.

"Ah, Klinq's new little friend. She sounds intriguing," he voiced quickly before adding, "She doesn't sound like a lover of dark things. You need to be careful with this one and I imagine knowing you, you are simply observing her."

"For the moment, yes," she agreed with him softly. "I had a strange energy following me today in the forest and on my way home, I saw this lovely young lady sneaking around outside our home. She says she was looking for Klinq but we both know there is no such thing as coincidence."

He nodded in agreement. "It is a wise move to keep her close and pay attention to what she is doing after what happened today. An energy followed you? What type of energy was it?" he asked, curious at this latest development of events.

Astrid often questioned Isra on energetic and magical components as he wanted to make sure she was safe.

7

She recalled back to earlier when she'd felt the energy, closing her eyes in order to recapture the vivid moment in her mind.

"It was strong and powerful. It wanted me to go to it but I resisted its forceful energies," she explained.

Astrid looked at her with a serious look on his face, especially in his eyes. "It most likely saw you as a threat and if the young girl downstairs has anything linked to this incident, we will find out and deal with it *and* her."

He kissed her forehead. She loved when he spoke like this; he was so strong and assertive. Astrid had a power about him, an indication; when he said something, something in his voice told you that whatever he'd said was real and that he was being serious. She loved it when he took control; he had so much strength and mental agility.

It was getting cooler. Isra glanced toward the window and saw that the sun was about to set. She remembered Contessia was still in her living room.

She softly whispered in his ear, "I still have a lady to entertain downstairs. You distracted me with your strength and masculine energy and I've totally forgotten about leaving her down there."

Astrid chuckled and whispered back, "I hope I was a good distraction."

She reached out and kissed him one more time, lingering on his lips to savor the moment as she slowly breathed, "Oh yes, you are. Always."

She pulled away from him and got to her feet. He immediately got up and followed her as she turned to leave the room. She carried on and headed toward the stairs as he slowly moved to her. He came up from behind and wrapped his arms around her waist, holding on to her tight.

"Oh, you thought you could just get away from me, did you?" he questioned playfully as she allowed him to plant his kiss on her lips once more.

She laughed and was flirtatious in her response. "I have to entertain. Contessia will be wondering where I am. She must be so scared to be in such a place of darkness."

She sniggered as Astrid gave her a sly smile. "Yes, and I bet you are loving that," he joked. "I will come down, but I will make myself scarce."

He waved a finger and began to concentrate. She stared at him intensely as he worked with the energies and after a few seconds, he was raven again. Nicely disguised and perfect to go and keep an eye on the newcomer and to also allow him to be close to his lover without anyone being any the wiser. Only Isra would know his true identity.

She smiled at his newly changed raven appearance and held out her arm for him to cling onto her. She came down the steps with Astrid happily sitting on her shoulder, grinning at her from ear to ear. Feeling dignified, she entered the room.

Contessia was on the couch, the same place she had been before Isra had left and uttered a small fake smile when the witch entered the room which amused Isra greatly. She smiled back because she sensed the girl's fear and laughed at this to herself. It made her feel very powerful to know that another felt the need to put on a performance in order to satisfy her.

She greeted the girl with a friendly gesture. "More tea, my dear?" she asked sweetly.

Contessia quickly replied, "Oh yes, please. That would be lovely. I am so thirsty." She then added, "This may be a redundant question, but where is Klinq? He seems to have disappeared."

Lady Isra had seen Klinq leave their presence earlier and thought to herself, *Oh, he is cowering in the basement, poor weak-minded little gnome,* but then she remembered Contessia was waiting for her answer.

She absently replied, "I am not too certain on where he is. Perhaps he needed a rest and retreated to his quarters."

Contessia, feeling a little relieved, sat up straight on the couch and responded, "Yes, that makes sense, he seemed tired earlier on. I hope he isn't working himself too hard for you."

Lady Isra heard the comment and silently chuckled before adding, "Oh, I am sure his physical health is just fine. I wouldn't ask him to do something if he was unwell or in low spirits."

The girl was cautious and concerned for her friend. *How sweet,* she thought sarcastically as she was keenly interested to see what developed between Klinq and Contessia.

Now that she had Contessia here, she intended to keep her here for the time being. She saw it was getting dark and this only contributed to her plan.

She turned to Contessia and softly remarked, "It is getting very late, and I don't want you having to go outside in the dark to get home, so you may stay in my company tonight."

Contessia realized she wasn't getting home any time soon.

She mumbled awkwardly, "Okay, I guess that will be fine. But where will I sleep?" she asked curiously. She realized she didn't know her way around the building at all and didn't want to get lost or end up somewhere she shouldn't.

The last thing she would want to do is discover some unwanted nasties in a witch's tower. She was a witch herself, but this is something she wanted to avoid. She didn't want to get into anything she couldn't get out of without some excessive force.

Lady Isra suddenly realized she hadn't been thinking about her proposition and admitted thoughtfully, "Oh my, I never gave that much consideration. Hmmm. We have another bedroom at the top of the tower. It is a little dusty as it hasn't been occupied for some time, but there are no leaks or drafts so you will pass the night peacefully."

Contessia considered the prospect. She didn't know her way around this place but it was a slightly better offer than having to walk home to her clan through the dark forest. Who knows what kind of horrid sights could materialize while she was out there?

"Well okay, it is not what I had in mind, but I guess for tonight it will suffice my needs."

Lady Isra looked ecstatic at this notion. She would be staying the night and would be under the witch's full control. *Oh, what a splendid night it will be!* Isra thought to herself with an evil smile.

There was just one problem; there was no spare bedroom in the tower. She collected her thoughts and envisioned the tower in all its glory, taking into account the building structure, and then all of its rooms in sheer detail so she had a clear map of the tower in her mind.

Isra then closed her eyes and visualized carefully what she wanted to create: a nice, dark, dank room with an antique four poster bed draped with white sheets with antique oak furniture carefully placed around the room in a messy format. She wanted it to look like it was untidy and messy, like it had long been abandoned by its former occupant.

She looked at the new bedroom, pleased with her hard work, and then magically conjured up a door for it before adding some dust and dirt for good measure. The room looked incredibly realistic. Something else was added to this; unbeknownst to Isra, in addition to her marvelous creation she had just whipped up.

I won't tell you what it is at this time, but I can promise you that what was created was grotesque and horrifying. The best way I can describe it is like something out of a nightmare. Contessia was in for one hell of a surprise.

8

Well, it was settled. Contessia had agreed to Lady Isra's request to stay the night.

Lady Isra gently placed her hand on Contessia's shoulder and sweetly explained, "Astrid will take you to your room where you will spend the night. If you should need anything, you know where to find me."

Contessia simply looked on as Isra spoke, not knowing what to make of the witch's remark. She wasn't sure if Isra was being nice and sweet or just being sweetly false to impress her.

Isra then looked at Astrid fondly as he sat on her shoulder and looking at Contessia directly, she whispered, "Keep her safe and warm, my precious one," and she watched as he cawed loudly and flew next to Contessia.

Astrid circled her and cawed loudly as she stared at him in bewilderment; she wasn't expecting her guide to be a raven. Isra stood behind Contessia and she watched Astrid fly in front of her as he led her up the stairs to what some might say could be her doom. Contessia walked slowly behind Astrid as he flew up the stairs and led her to the bedroom that Isra had magically created. She seemed curious, interested in this place that she was spending the night, instead of her usual woodland cottage she lived in with members of her clan.

It was a change of scenery for her; something in it captivated her —the bold, dark colors, the rich décor—it avidly stimulated her imagination. She was a witch herself but she had never been in such a rich, vivid world like she was tonight as she was occupying the tower of Lady Isra of the Dark.

She entered the room cautiously, making sure the door was closed behind her and sat on the old four poster bed. Everything in here was old, tattered, and looked rather damaged. She liked the old feel, but felt like this room wasn't quite as it appeared.

She didn't get much time to explore it; she was tired and was falling asleep on the four poster bed before she could ponder any more of her wild thoughts. Astrid saw she was falling asleep so he quietly jumped on the bed and whispered something in her ear, then as quick as he had done so, he left the room without uttering a word.

Astrid soon swiftly materialized into his normal human appearance and headed into his and Isra's bedroom where she sat at the dresser, perusing spells. Much to his amusement, he snuck up behind her, careful to not make a sound, and grabbed her from behind which resulted in making her jump.

"Arghhhhhhhhh!" she exclaimed loudly as she realized it was Astrid that had sneaked up behind her.

"Hahaha, sorry but I just couldn't resist!" he joked playfully, admiring the result of his handiwork, a much-jerked Isra. She wasn't scared, but she had almost jumped out of her skin thanks to Astrid's little trick.

"You got me good. Now, is there anything else up your sleeve for tonight?" She questioned her lover playfully as he took her away from the dresser and carried her onto the bed, where he proceeded to passionately kiss her.

She had no control; he had her pinned on the bed. She didn't know how to react, as she was so used to being in control.

He paused silently and then admitted, "Well, I do have a few things lined up, but some will have to wait."

He was being cryptic, and she wondered what he was referring to. Her wonder soon melted away as he kissed her again, gently massaging her tongue with his. Her mind had been stopped once again. He had a habit of doing this. He was able to turn off all her thoughts with just one single touch of his lips.

"Hmmm, I can't possibly imagine what those things will be," she said with a whimsical smile.

He kissed her lips again, keeping her locked in his grip as he passionately embraced her. She continued to allow him to fill her with passion and had forgotten about her houseguest this evening ... but someone had not.

Contessia was fast asleep in the bedroom; it was dark and there was nobody present to disturb her. She slept peacefully and looked very content. Not a soul could have awakened her.

All of a sudden, there was a loud bang that sounded like a human fist pounding on her bedroom door. She immediately jerked awake at the sound of it. Her first instinct was to check that she was the only occupant in the bedroom, and then she walked slowly toward the door and opened it to see if anyone was outside. Again, there was nobody.

This was all very strange, and she didn't understand it. It was quite baffling to her. Who could have made the banging sound when there was nobody to be seen in the hallway?

She decided to explore this odd occurrence further and proceeded to walk down the hallway, looking behind her as she walked. She was a little frightened and it would be safe to say on edge at this point. She wasn't used to strange things happening to her. This was a new experience but something in her curiosity made her go further into the darkness to find what had disturbed her.

She seemed somewhat hypnotized as she walked down the dark hallway, holding onto the wall for support. There were no lights, only small candles lighting the way as she slowly walked down the hallway. She finally came to the end of the hallway and saw a wooden door with a glass window. The frame was dusty and covered in cobwebs. Cobwebs covered the entire door so no one had been near this place for many moons she thought as she picked some of the dust off her finger.

The glass had been shattered and destroyed. Broken shards of glass were everywhere, completely covering the cold stone floor. It was lucky she was wearing shoes or she would have been cut to pieces.

She touched the door with her hand and then moved it away again. A voice in her head told her to turn back and go back to her room, but Contessia was already captivated by this dirty, dusty door and she was going to walk through it no matter what the voice inside her said.

She opened the door cautiously. It squeaked a little at the hinges; it must have been very old, she thought to herself as she closed it behind her.

She saw a passageway appear in front of her. It was small and narrow. She looked back one last time and walked toward it and there she noticed a stone staircase which was covered in yet more dust. She started to make her way down the steps and was only on the second step when she suddenly looked horrified at the scene surrounding her.

Spider webs with spiders in each web blocked the space between the wall and the steps.

She stood back in sheer horror. She tried to immediately run back up but as she got to the top of the staircase, she noticed that the wooden door now had three wooden planks placed firmly across it, blocking it so there was no escape.

These had appeared as if by magic. There was no other explanation for how they had got there. The only way out was to go down the steps with the spiders in their webs. Each web had a different spider. There was one that was orange, another was green, and some black and in other colors. She counted them several times, hoping she would be wrong, but in this instance she wasn't. She tried to scream and stop looking at them but she couldn't.

Inside, she was screaming but no sound was coming out of her mouth. She had no choice but to brave the terrible spiders that had appeared out of nowhere, blocking her way down the grotesque staircase that seemed like something out of a nightmare.

She cringed as she walked down each step, taking great care not to disturb the spider webs with the spiders in them and hoping and praying that they would not disturb her.

Today was not her lucky day. The orange spider took a liking to Contessia and moved from its web, slowly onto her face. She screamed in anguish! She couldn't believe what was happening.

"Arggg!! Get away from me!" she cried out as the orange spider crawled in her hair and down her neck.

It was vile. She could feel it climbing inside her nightgown. She wanted this freaky nightmare to be over and so she started running, running as fast as she could. The orange spider still climbing inside her nightgown was shaken off her and she continued running.

She felt herself all over in a panic, checking to see if any other unwanted intruders had decided to get friendly with her. She found nothing, but her skin crawled with the feeling of the spider on her. Finally, feeling relieved, she saw another door and headed straight for it, hoping this was the end of her nightmare.

She didn't hesitate and opened the door. To her surprise, she was back inside the tower, only it looked different from this angle. She looked carefully; directly opposite her, there was a small room next to a staircase, and opposite that was a large, heavy door which looked like the main door to the tower.

She was standing in the hallway and there was another staircase. It was in fact the staircase she had climbed earlier to get to the room where she had tea with Lady Isra. She looked confused as the door she had come through to get to this part of the building had disappeared into thin air.

Paying closer attention to the room in front of her, she noticed it was dank and smelled musty. She looked closer and she saw clearly it was the basement where Klinq lived and slept.

Feeling the need for a friend right now, still feeling shaken up from her experience, she pounded on his door and shouted, "KLINQ, PLEASE WAKE UP!"

He awoke from his sleep and came to the door, looking tired with his hair creeping out from under his hat. He saw his friend Contessia, noticing her state of panic as he let her in. He was worried and concerned for her.

She immediately hugged him tightly and cried. "I have had the most terrifying experience of my life! I can't get over it!" she exclaimed as Klinq tried to understand why she was upset.

He held her, although feeling extremely awkward as he was much shorter than her at just three feet tall, so quite a difference.

"What happened to you? You're shaking!" he asked her.

She began to hyperventilate; her experience was unnerving and even though it was all over, she still felt it in every zone of her body. It was gross, and she could still feel spiders all over her even though she knew they were long gone. She breathed heavily, trying to contain her breath despite her panic. It was overwhelming her greatly.

"I was woken up by something, so I went out in the hallway to see what it was..."

"And?"

She didn't finish that sentence as the horror of it, walking down those steps after that dark tunnel to be greeted with those spiders everywhere, replayed in her mind again. God, it made her shiver all over. She wished she had a blanket around her right now as she stood shivering and mortified.

"And what?!" Klinq asked her as he held her and sat her down on his bed. "What happened, Contessia?"

"There was a tunnel after the hallway came to an end and I saw a door with some stairs, so I opened it and walked through. I started to go down the stairs all of a sudden..."

She stopped again; this was tormenting her.

It had her and she didn't know what would happen next. She knew she had made a bad mistake in coming here. She knew now she had to find a way out. This trail of thought had stopped again because she was so scared.

She thought to herself, *Okay, I hate dark things but this was more than I could have ever imagined. This is a grotesque world of evil and nobody is safe in its presence.*

Klinq noticed her pause again but said nothing and sat next to her, comforting her with a hot cup of tea which she accepted and began to drink slowly. Still reliving the horror of what had happened, she began to speak again.

"I go down the stairs and these spiders are everywhere, all across the stairs. I have never seen so many spiders in my entire life." She gasped and began to cry once again. "I tried to go back up the stairs and run the hell out of that door but the door had been blocked with three planks of wood. No idea how that happened, but it was as if it was magic!"

She continued tearfully as Klinq listened. "I then had no choice but to brave those spiders. I did all I could to not disturb them, but one jumped on me and oh my goodness, Klinq, it went in my hair, inside my night dress. It was a living hell and one I do not want to repeat ever again!"

She sobbed wildly on his arm.

Klinq thought carefully about Contessia's story and he had to admit he didn't understand it. He didn't know much about things of this nature, but this was something he had not planned for. This was something horrific and now he was thinking on how he could keep *himself* out of the shit, as cowardly as he was. He wanted to be nowhere near what was happening despite his feelings for Contessia which were emerging more clearly by the day.

Contessia suddenly stood up, faced the wall while rooted to the spot and stayed silent before responding, "I am in way too deep here. I have to go. I am sorry."

She turned to leave and promptly left Klinq bewildered at her exit.

9

ontessia found her way back to the bedroom she was
staying in and stayed awake as the night died and watched
the sun rise.

She couldn't sleep after her ordeal. She didn't want to sleep. Her
mind was far too occupied with thoughts. Thoughts of fear, thoughts
of what she had gotten herself into by entering the tower of Lady Isra,
and thoughts of being defeated and being out of her depth. It was
that last one that crippled her.

She knew about magic, yes she did. Her clan had taught her well
in many aspects of Wicca and magic and she had proven to be a
strong and resourceful young witch in her lifetime; however, dark
magic was something she had no experience in and now she felt
frightened and scared.

She didn't know what to do. She was scared of what would
happen next as she sat on the bed, clutching her stomach and
watching the sun slowly appear for what would be the start of
another day. She made her way downstairs. She had stayed in this
room for long enough and slowly held onto the wall as she passed
through to the main room in the tower.

The room was empty, but a candle was lit by the window. It

flickered wildly with bright orange flames as she entered the room. She was a little unnerved but decided to make herself some tea and relax as she wanted to figure things out.

She sat by the window and watched the candle. It seemed to hypnotize her as she let her finger hover above its deep orange flame and it enticingly danced around it. It gave her a sense of peace as the flame touched her finger but did not burn it. She was in a trance state with it; her mind was starting to loosen and she felt a loss of control.

She realized what was happening—this was yet another act of magic grabbing her fiercely—she tried to free herself from the trance by moving her finger but as she did, the flame hit her skin with a burning sensation and she was immediately returned to her normal conscious state.

She whined in pain and exclaimed, "Oww, that hurt!" as she pulled herself away from the candle, touching her finger softly in an attempt to soothe the stinging pain.

She picked up her tea and moved over to the couch where she waited for several hours for signs of life to erupt from the household. She watched a small clock on the wall as it ticked and she felt her hands getting clammy and beads of sweat appear on her forehead as she nervously waited for someone to appear.

She was just finishing her third cup of tea when a noise could be heard from behind the door.

She turned around as she watched it open and walked Astrid in his human form. She had not met him yet and had only seen him in his raven form, so she was shocked to see such a tall, dark and handsome stranger appear before her.

He noticed her sitting on the couch as he shut the door behind him and spoke formally, "Oh, I am sorry, I didn't know anybody was in here," he said apologetically.

His eyes met hers and Contessia smiled as she relaxed her body on the couch and answered, "It's okay, I have been up for a few hours. I don't sleep well in strange places."

She realized she didn't know who she was talking to and was curious to know who this stranger was.

He laughed and joked, "Ah sleep, who needs that?"

The raven-man was looking disheveled as he poured himself a glass of water, wearing a black shirt revealing black underwear covering himself below.

Contessia looked at him, intrigued, and couldn't help but stare at his immaculate and well-muscled body as he took a large gulp from the water glass. Astrid noticed Contessia staring at him and his cheeks reddened as he felt the power of her stare on his body. He introduced himself in a friendly manner but didn't smile.

"I am so rude, I must apologize. I am Astrid, Isra's lover. She is still asleep, and I did not wish to wake her from her slumber."

He gulped the rest of the water and placed the glass on a table. Contessia continued staring at him.

He looked at Contessia thoughtfully and lowered his voice. "I didn't expect to find anybody down here."

"Neither did I," she said slowly.

She was puzzled and perplexed. This man was a raven yesterday and now she was seeing him as a man. It confused her. This was the man who had shown her to her room, but just in a different form. She resisted the temptation to ask him questions and sipped her tea instead.

He noticed her perplexed behavior and asked, "So, what is a young girl like yourself doing alone sipping tea just as the sun has risen?"

His question was full of curiosity and wonder, but he knew she couldn't help but answer him. She narrowed her eyes at him, watching his eyes slowly as she thought about the question. After a moment's pause, she replied, "I didn't have the best of nights. I came here to calm down after my horrific experience upstairs."

He met her stare with a sly but yet wicked smile. Astrid noticed the fear in Contessia's voice as he responded, "Horrific experience? My, you must have really been through something."

He quickly turned away as he feared he was soon to laugh at her misfortune. Now he was facing the wall and could hold his laughter. He wanted to laugh at this girl Contessia badly but resisted the urge to make fun of her "horrific experience," as she had worded it. He made himself look busy by fiddling with a teacup.

He was still facing the wall when he added, "I hope it wasn't too painful."

Contessia was taken aback by this response and she held herself in a protective way as the memory began to resurface for her. She shook and she shivered at the very thought. She wished there could have been pain. Pain wasn't a word she would use for the tunnel of horror she had found herself in last night when she had wandered out of her room after a noise had distracted her.

Pain would have been a blessing, she thought to herself grimly as she felt her shoulders tense with panic, checking for unwanted guests as she relived the moment when the spider landed on her face.

Thankfully, her shoulder was bare and she was okay for the present moment. Relieved, she sat back on the couch and relaxed. She thought back to Astrid's response and pondered why this stranger would be so interested in what had happened to her.

She thought to herself, *Why is he asking me this? Why is he being so friendly about it? Why is it so interesting to him?*

None of the questions she could answer, but she had to answer the raven-man's questions with some dignified response because he was going to ask her again if she didn't. She hadn't known him for more than a few minutes but already she knew that he was the lover of Lady Isra and that he had a dark, sinister side to him. One that made her more than a little nervous which she couldn't help but show as she tried to keep eye contact with him. She stared at him, feeling inadequate with herself.

She then murmured weakly, "There was no pain, but I wish there would have been. This was horrific, something I don't think I will ever forget!"

He took interest in her experience; this was apparent when he asked her. "What the hell happened to you?" Astrid sounded sincere but he was just curious. He wanted to know what could have made a young witch such as Contessia so weak and infirm.

She stood up and turned to face the raven-man and began to utter the words from her mouth. "I was woken from a restful sleep to a noise outside my room, so naturally, I went to see what it was. I followed it until I came to a tunnel and a door, which I entered and it revealed a staircase."

She felt weak as she spoke, and Astrid noticed how weary she was as she told her tale.

She continued slowly, "I got to the first step and started to make my way down, but to my horror, the entire staircase was surrounded by spiders. The whole place was covered in them, they were everywhere and the door had been blocked so I had no choice but to face the disgusting creatures that had so cruelly blocked my way."

As she finished, her breathing became very shallow and she felt her heart race furiously. Her body reminded her of her trauma. She held her hands to her chest as she tried to calm herself which failed greatly as her heart continued to thump wildly inside her chest in such a way that she felt it might burst.

She looked at Astrid for sympathy, hoping that something in him might show her some empathy. This was not to be as he showed a voided reaction to her story. The raven-man simply turned away as Contessia was in her state of panic. A cold and callous gesture on his part, but he felt personally that this was not a matter that concerned him so he chose not to be involved.

Contessia noticed his change in behavior and how cold he was and asked, "Why did you turn away? Did I do something to offend you?"

He laughed slyly as he retorted, "No, but small matters of humans do not concern me. I bid you well. Goodbye for now."

And with that, he swiftly exited the room and closed the door behind him.

Contessia stood up at once and left the room, running down the steps with her hand clutching her chest and looking frantically for the door out of this place. She'd had enough of the darkness and strange occurrences here. She wanted to go home.

She looked all over to find a door, worried more than ever now that something else would happen in this fortress of evil she had been introduced to. She saw the door at last and ran to it quickly as her breath ran away with her. She banged on it, tugging at the handle and to her disappointment, it did not open. She tried again, banging it and pounding it with her fist, hoping the supreme force might somehow make it unlock.

She then took a step back and then ran toward it, forcing her entire body against it in an attempt to push it open. To her surprise, this time it opened automatically. She thought for a moment that the door may have been magically enchanted like everything else in this forsaken place, but that thought left her as she found herself in the fresh air outside. She saw the grass and trees in the grounds and began to relax as her ordeal was now over.

10

Contessia took residence on the grass and lay on it, feeling the blades touch her skin as she felt her breath and heart rate return to their normal states. She laid there in tranquil serenity for a few minutes as the sun's rays bathed her in their healing light.

She noticed how bright and warm it was and how readjusted she felt after her ordeal in that tower where she had met Lady Isra and the raven Astrid who turned out to be a man. She wasn't fond of dark forces; she had been taught to stay away from any kind of evil, but she had gone to the tower as she had been worried about Klinq, the gnome she had met only two days ago in the forest.

She and Klinq had become great friends and after she had been told he worked for a witch who was evil, she had extended her hand of friendship to the cowardly gnome who had hidden behind a tree to avoid being seen by the Wiccan girl, which had failed greatly as she had spotted him.

Her entire body felt lighter since she had been laying here in the grass, so she sat up and stared at the bright wonder in the sky as she felt good about herself and thought about nothing but going home. She wanted to say goodbye to Klinq but something in her had decided against it. She felt bad about this, but she didn't want anything else to happen to her or him.

She felt that if she went back there, something else would happen and it wouldn't just be her in the firing line. She didn't want anything to happen to Klinq. Yes, a witch had decided she was an enemy but her heart sank at the thought of anything happening to her friend.

And in her heart, he was much more than just her friend...

She had feelings for the gnome and that didn't make the decision to not say goodbye any easier. She felt cruel and callous to herself but she saw no other way of keeping both her and Klinq safe from the witch's evil ways.

Contessia was just about to head home when she heard rustling in the grass blades, and noticed something slowly moving toward her. She stood up, paying close attention to the intrusion. She noted the noise and listened carefully.

She closed her eyes in order to try and zone in on whatever it was, fearing it may be an attack like the one that had befallen her the night before and she upped all her defenses. Her body was poised like a well-made set of armor as she stood rigid and tall.

The attacker emerged from its hidden shelter in the grass and pounced on her, knocking Contessia to the ground at once as it hit her with its entire body weight, stopping her from being able to get back up. She opened her eyes to see a gigantic black cat sat upon her. It was furious and growled at her. She noticed its fur was standing on end because of the rage it possessed as it stared at her. She noted its fury and then something made her glance at the sky—she didn't know what—but as she did, a lightning flash cascaded over her and the gigantic cat returned to its normal kitten size.

Contessia gasped in horror and couldn't believe her eyes. The thing that had just attacked her was a kitten and it was now meowing at her feet, most likely calling for its owner. She turned to scream at yet another thing happening, but was stopped as Lady Isra stood by, watching the little kitten and cooing at him.

She stared at the black kitten and spoke softly with much

admiration for the little one. "Why, I've been looking everywhere for you!"

Contessia tried to work out how Lady Isra had gotten there and how she was linked to the kitten that had just attacked her under a much bigger and scarier form. She looked at Lady Isra as she picked up the tiny kitten and cradled it in her arms, mystified at how it had changed from huge to tiny in a matter of moments. Perhaps she was crazy. Perhaps she had imagined the entire incident, but maybe, just maybe like everything else, it had been magically enhanced!

I mean after all, this *was* the tower of a witch and where a witch could be found, there would also be magic! She knew magic was involved somewhere.

She approached Lady Isra boldly and exclaimed, "That ferocious beast just attacked me!"

Lady Isra began to laugh at the frightened girl's remark. "Nonsense, child! He is just a baby." Lady Isra cooed at the tiny kitten.

Contessia looked enraged and shouted at the witch, "Well, he wasn't a baby a few minutes ago when he attacked me!"

Lady Isra gently put Onyx down on the ground and grabbed Contessia by the arm as she announced, "Okay, I have had enough of your human crap for one day! He is a baby, he did *not* attack you."

There was a small pause as Onyx rubbed himself around Isra's legs and she smiled as he happily did so, but then remembered she had a hold of Contessia and looked at her solemnly.

She then started to speak slowly but firmly. "I think you should seek some kind of help; you are hallucinating, my child!"

She let the girl fall to the ground with an almighty thud and carefully looked down at her as Contessia tried to maintain a sense of focus of what was happening. Contessia could not believe it. She had just been accused of being crazy by Lady Isra. She was not crazy! That small black kitten was gigantic, at least ten times its kitten size and it had attacked her!

The witch must be doing this, she thought, *she must be. She is doing all she can to make my life a sheer misery. Maybe she and the raven-man are in this together; perhaps it's all happening to me because doing this gives them pleasure. Perhaps I am their toy!*

The ludicrous thoughts whirled around in Contessia's head over and over as she tried to lift herself up. The fall had weakened her and she struggled to regain her composure.

This was crazy! All of it! The entire charade had been a disaster for Contessia from start to finish. This was true as the moment Contessia had entered the tower of Lady Isra, things had gone awry; she had been hypnotized, tortured mentally, and taunted for her fears and now attacked by Lady Isra's cat, Onyx.

She finally lifted herself up and looked around to see Klinq sheepishly hiding behind the witch.

He stood behind Lady Isra and was hidden by her long black cloak that dragged on the ground as Lady Isra stood there. Klinq was dressed in his usual attire, ragged clothes and his hair poking out from under his hat.

He couldn't even look at Contessia. He couldn't stand up for her. He was such a cowardly creature and Contessia could now see it.

She folded her arms in an act of defense and exclaimed, "I am *not* crazy! I am *not* hallucinating about anything, let alone the things I have experienced here!"

Her long purple hair gently moved to one side of her face and she brushed it out of the way as she looked at Klinq directly in the eye and started again.

"And you. You can't even look at me! What is wrong with you? Why are you such a coward? Hiding behind a witch and a dark, evil one at that!" she inquired angrily as she stood waiting for an answer.

He didn't speak for a while and stared mindlessly at the floor.

Contessia wasn't happy about this and so she launched into a tirade as she faced him. "I came here to see you Klinq, to see if you were okay. And ever since I got here, I have been attacked, tortured and tormented. Is there anything you can say for yourself in your defense?"

Klinq looked at her silently, and then mumbled, "I don't have control over any of that. I am staying out of it. Sorry."

He ran back into the tower which pleased Lady Isra greatly. She had a huge beaming grin on her face as Contessia stood shell-shocked at his lack of support for her.

Lady Isra smiled wickedly at Contessia and sneered, "Well, it looks like you are on your own with this one. Klinq is not going to help you. Neither will anyone else."

She paused as she sniggered and looked at Contessia. She glanced at her tower and the majestic sights in front of her and the grounds as she thought to herself about what she had become. She took stock of her achievements; now she had everything she wanted, she was totally in control.

She eyed Contessia carefully and knew exactly what she was, a weak Wiccan girl with too many temptations. Oh, this girl would regret ever coming into contact with Isra. Yes, she had decided on it. She had a new toy to play with and she would design this perfectly. She knew how easy it would be for her to manipulate Contessia and get her to do exactly what she wanted.

Contessia stared at Lady Isra in return and waited for the witch to speak; she knew something was coming next that she would not enjoy hearing. She upped her defenses and straightened her body so her posture was the same as the witch's and listened intently.

Lady Isra noticed the girl's concentration and laughed. "Well, you have no friends here. Klinq won't stand up for you, but let's not give that idiot any energy as I have a proposition for you, my child."

Contessia—taken aback at this—asked cautiously, "A proposition? What kind?"

Lady Isra walked over to the girl, placed her hand on her shoulder and whispered, "A chance to be what you've heard so much about but were so callously warned not to be."

Contessia imagined this and was curious at the potential of it and what it would ultimately mean for ultimately. Would it be good, or would it be evil?

Contessia asked Lady Isra calmly, "What do you want?"

Lady Isra smiled and whispered excitedly, "I like you. You have something in. Join me here and learn about the dark ways under my wing."

Contessia pondered this notion. "You want to teach me the dark arts?" she asked before silently smiling, her grin as big as the sun. "Actually, the dark arts are something I've long been afraid of."

Lady Isra laughed. "Yes, I know dear, you fear all dark things, but darkness is in YOU!" She finished sweetly.

She looked so wise when she talked about darkness and what it did to those it captured. She definitely knew what she was talking about. You could see it in her, the passion, the splendor, the wisdom and the power. Never forget the power, because the power won't ever forget you!

Contessia looked at Isra again and a glimmer appeared, a bright glow that radiated her all over. It made her purple hair shine, and the Wiccan girl suddenly had a sense of enlightenment ... but surely this couldn't have come from something dark?

Contessia had thought about the witch's words: *Darkness is in YOU!* She had to admit, the witch had a point and it was very much true to her upbringing; she had spent a long time trying to fight the darkness around her.

Contessia had been warned by her clan members to stay away from dark forces and anything that came with them. She had been told that it was bad and unhealthy but now something was telling her it was okay. She didn't know enough about it to understand, but she felt like she had a green light paving the way to this new path in life and something was telling her to take it.

She didn't have a real home, not really. Her clan had taken care of her and raised her well in the Wiccan ways but it wasn't a home. It was just a way of life for now, something to live by until something better came along. And now something better has come along.

The question was, would the shy Wiccan girl take it?

Power being handed on a plate didn't happen every day. This was rare and not something to be scoffed at. But Lady Isra's intentions were far from good; however, Contessia was not aware of just how murky things were about to become.

She suddenly saw a different side of the witch, one that showed kindness and wisdom in wanting to help the young. She didn't for one second suspect that there would be darkness and hatred involved in this grand plan. Nevertheless, Contessia was seriously pondering Lady Isra's offer! To be a witch and to harness and grow her power, much more than she had done before. To her, it was an opportunity of a lifetime and also one that had great temptation.

The Wiccan girl stood with her hair blowing in the wind and announced excitedly, "Okay, I accept your proposition!"

11

Lady Isra took the young girl by the hand, looking very excited as she said, "Come, child, we have much work to do."

And she hurried away with Contessia into her tower. There would be no telling just what Isra was going to be doing with Contessia as she disappeared into the tower with her so quickly, but you can bet your life it wouldn't benefit Klinq in any way.

Klinq, who had gone back down to his dingy basement, was not aware of this latest development as he had cowardly snuck away as soon as he could. He didn't want to be involved in the dealings with Isra and Contessia. His friend had seen his true nature and had quite rightly scolded him for it and also confronted him for his behavior in which he had not stood up for her.

Isra had seen this dispute between Contessia and Klinq as an opportunity and she had made Contessia an offer to learn the dark arts with her in her tower, an offer Contessia had gratefully accepted much to Lady Isra's sheer pleasure and amusement, knowing she would exploit the innocent Wiccan girl.

Contessia was not aware of this part of the plan of course, and Lady Isra had given Klinq clear instructions to stay away from her protégé from here on. Klinq had an inkling of what was going to happen, but he was far too fearful of Lady Isra to go against her request, so he stayed in his basement, carefully watched by Astrid who sat outside Klinq's basement door.

Astrid had disappeared for the duration of the day's activities. He wanted to be unseen. He wasn't entirely sure of what Isra was up to, but then he did have his own ideas and didn't need confirmation from the witch herself on her festivities involving Contessia.

He was sure enough that something bad was about to happen to the pretentious and incredibly stupid girl who had chosen to join forces with Lady Isra. Astrid waited until all was quiet with Klinq and reemerged in his manly human form; taking care to make sure he wasn't noticed as he changed his appearance and stood next to an ornate gold mirror.

He admired himself in the mirror while focusing on the image of Contessia, her purple hair swaying back and forth. As he held the image of her in his mind, he whispered, "Follow her. Follow the girl. Keep her insane. Keep her alive and well because now she is under my spell."

He flashed a triumphant smile as he finished and grinned as the whole tower began to shake violently. Just after Astrid uttered that final word, a vivid flash of green lightning struck above the mirror and encircled the whole tower, encasing everything in green as a malevolent power surged and echoed throughout the atmospheric space between Astrid and the mirror.

The tower shook violently, causing everyone inside to stay perfectly still as the lightning took its hold and traveled to the main room of the tower and slowly stopped as it reached its destination: Contessia.

Contessia stood dumbstruck, not knowing what to do. She was alone and helpless. Lady Isra was nowhere to be seen, another small detail that made this the perfect moment to target Contessia.

Ablaze with shimmering hues of emerald green, the powerful energy lingered in a frenzy as it hovered above her waist and surveyed every part of her. It then raised upward, starting slowly and then finally callously hitting Contessia sharply in the heart to which she clutched her chest and fell hopelessly to the ground. Her whole chest began to feel as if it were on fire as the fiery lightning blast penetrated her heart.

She was motionless on the ground, searching relentlessly for the will to open her eyes but to no avail as the energy that was now inside her had her completely paralyzed.

Astrid then appeared and inspected the motionless and lifeless Contessia proudly as he pondered her loss of consciousness. He smiled evilly and muttered, "She is alone and out of the wilderness and now I get to have some fun."

Astrid bent down next to Contessia and inspected his handiwork. Her eyes were closed and her body was solid, as if she were dead. He moved his hand to her chest and let it hover over her weakened heart. It had been severely weakened from the lightning blast. She wouldn't be able to move for a few hours. He felt her energy with his hands and gently shut off every defensive nerve in her body. She would be completely under his evil control now that he had initiated this crucial move to disarm her.

He then stood still and focused on her body as he signaled the energy to move Contessia so that it was as if she was in a blissful sleep by lifting his finger. He called upon the energies needed to carry out his task.

Admiring the lifeless and sleeping girl for a moment, he paused as he noticed a thick clump of purple hair that had covered the right side of her face and gently moved it back in place over to her fringe. Poor girl hadn't even had time to take care of her wayward hair as the evil raven-man's spell conquered her.

Astrid suddenly heard Lady Isra's voice calling him from midair. She wasn't nearby; however green sparks appeared before him to signal her presence. She was in the air, mystically calling him. She had many talents and being everywhere at once or even in midair was certainly one of them.

Her voice echoed in the air with mystic green sparkles as she called, "Astrid, where are you? Come seek me!"

She called out softly but he detected perplexity in her voice. He immediately abandoned his current victim and listened to the voice to where his lover would be.

The last thing he wanted right now was to be caught torturing Contessia behind Isra's back. He didn't know how she would react, but he did know Isra had her own plans for the ill-fated Contessia and perhaps Astrid getting involved would not be the best idea for him to partake in at this moment in time.

He followed the green sparks of energy out of the door and down the staircase that led to the wooden tower door, and then stopped as he realized he was outside on the grounds. Thinking his lover would materialize, he prepared himself for her appearance to befall him while also hoping Isra had not seen him with Contessia.

A flash of violent lightning then came tumbling down from the night sky; the earth was fiery and covered in anger as lightning bolts cascaded down like bombs hitting the earth. Astrid lay in wait for something to emerge from the darkness that had brought this fiery sky shower, but it wasn't Lady Isra. Much to Astrid's surprise, a figure in a dark cloak burst out of nowhere, causing the earth to shake as the mystery being made its entrance known.

The figure lifted its hood and barked, "Well, this is nice! Not what I expected, but nice and quaint for someone who revels in evil-doing." She finished sarcastically, waving a finger at Astrid as she said, "Oh, I have no need for a man! Be gone, dear!"

Astrid took a step back as the figure lifted her hood further and revealed a woman with shoulder length golden hair that poked out of a solid black cloak; red was the focus on the sleeves and around the neckline. Her eyes flashed like fiery sapphire bullets that could kill you with one tainted look. Her violent entrance said she was full of rage and jealousy; bitterness was also apparent in her exterior as she walked less than regally.

Astrid stood with his arms folded toward the newcomer as he scowled. "Who the hell are *you* and what is your business in this world?"

She scoffed, "I have business with the one who used to be kind and good. Tell me, does she still reign?"

Something in her question told him she already knew the answer. Astrid immediately realized this was someone who was seeking out Isra and he formed a protective stance, his arms still folded, looking fearless as he challenged the stranger with his own question.

"Isra? Your business is with Lady Isra of the Dark?" he asked pointedly, noting her body language as she stared at him blindly.

Her hands were shaking as was her entire body. Something was bothering her, something she didn't appear to want to admit. Astrid assumed this meant she was hiding something about herself.

The venomous intruder remarked harshly, "Oh, so that is what she is calling herself these days?"

Astrid lowered his gaze and stared deeply into the vile creature's eyes to see what was inside and all he saw was bitterness and jealousy, followed by a sheer need for power and greed. Something he could see was inevitable by the way she presented herself out into the world. She was cold in her exterior and resented anyone doing better than she was doing herself. He could see the coldness in her heart, or more correctly, her lack of heart. It couldn't be beating if there was one.

He thoughtfully noted that her heart was cold because it had never been used and never had a purpose. This creature was someone nobody had any time for, nor did they want to give her their time; but yet she was standing here, seeking out his Isra and he did not like her one bit. So now he was even more determined to challenge her and her resistance made him even more motivated to do so.

"Yes, she is known as Lady Isra of the Dark! Now answer my question, who the hell are you and what do you want with Isra?"

He gave her the once-over, looking her up and down and saw there was nothing inside her to be feared. She was nothing special. She was just a lonely, desolate being. A being made of nothing. Nothing resided inside her but her bitter streak. The fiery show she'd put on by erupting her rage through the skies gave the illusion that she had power and was something to be feared but Astrid had very clearly seen through that.

He noted her defensive stance as she stood and answered his question in a sarcastic tone of voice. "I only want to talk to her. No malice or evil intent will come from me."

She finished quickly as the raven-man looked for the tiniest sign of a lie from her putrid lips. He was looking for the sign that she was being deceitful in her intent. He had his suspicions, but Astrid was a man of solid, hard proof and right now he needed that before making any moves that could be seen as dangerous and volatile.

He straightened himself up, easing some tension off his shoulders and piped up sharply, "Okay, you may speak with her, but let me commune with her first to make sure your arrival is welcome with Lady Isra."

It was at this point he realized the person calling to him, summoning him with the green energy was not Isra at all but at the time it had commenced, he thought it was. How stupid he had been to fall for that, he thought to himself as he examined the creature in black and red again before turning to leave the scene.

He nodded to the woman and said, "Follow me, but stay in the hallway until I give you the sign that it is okay to move from that spot."

He ordered her cautiously as he opened the heavy wooden door that gave access to Lady Isra of the Dark's tower.

He searched carefully for Isra, hoping to be able to get her alone in the silence in order to warn her about this stranger who he did not trust and did not even know her name. He scanned the main room for her; there was no sign of her. Contessia wasn't there either.

His guess was that Isra had found Contessia and taken her to her room. That was his best guess but anything could happen in this place. He decided he would go up to their bedroom in search of his love.

Astrid slowly climbed the staircase and poked his head around the door frame as he opened the door to his and Lady Isra's bedroom. She was quietly reading something on her desk, dressed in a purple silk nightgown with lace around the bosom and on the sleeves. She didn't even notice Astrid watching her as she slowly read the letters on the old, ornate pages of her book.

He snuck up behind her and laughed as he pounced out of nowhere, putting his hands on her back and watched as she almost jumped out of her skin and scolded him as she eyed him from behind her red framed glasses.

"Oh, for goodness sake Astrid, I am starting to think you do this to amuse yourself. Give me a warning the next time you have this silly idea in your head, please!"

He planted a kiss on her forehead while she gently pushed him away from her so she could move herself away from her desk.

He smiled, "Okay, I promise."

He grinned, pulling his witch closer to him and grabbing her gently yet also quite tightly so she couldn't push him away this time. He started to speak while kissing her slowly. "There is someone in the hallway that requests your presence. She is a bitter hag, dressed in red and black but she knows you by your first name only."

Isra stopped for a moment and began to think. Her thoughts now overtook her as she thought of all the people in her past ... and then it came to her.

Red and black, she thought, *and bitter too? Why, it can only be one,* she laughed to herself with a small sly smile. *Oh dear, I was hoping she'd wind up in the gutter or dead, but maybe she is inside,* she thought cheerfully as she laughed.

Astrid looked at Lady Isra who was still in her wild train of thought regarding her past memories, waiting for her to include him in her thoughts as he stood next to her, still holding her, waiting.

Ah yes, she remembered her well, and what a bitter old hag she was too.

Everilda was a bitter, self-righteous, know-it-all witch who had terrible ideas and an even more terrible mind. She was a loser at everything. She thought she had power but she was just too stupid and lacked imagination.

Isra had done better in her craft and was going beyond Everilda's level while fast making progress which greatly added to Everilda's jealousy of Isra and the power she possessed. Everilda had failed at every single spell and eventually lost her powers due to her own incompetence. She had created a potion—unsuccessfully of course—and it had turned the leader of the coven into a measly worm much to his disapproval.

Isra laughed as she fondly remembered this embarrassing defeat of Everilda. The grin on her face suggested that she enjoyed Everilda being defeated and that this wasn't the only incident in which Everilda had been humiliated.

Isra turned to Astrid thoughtfully, laughing as she boasted, "Oh, it could only be Everilda, the failure at life in all forms!"

Astrid pulled her closer to him again. He looked her in the eyes and speculated, "I had a feeling she was here for the wrong reasons but she wants to talk to you. I said I would check with you first as I don't want anyone hurting my beautiful witch!"

Isra held her hand out for the raven-man to kiss it gently and whispered, "Nobody can harm me. I wouldn't worry. She has no power!" Then she turned to Astrid with a mischievous smile and proposed, "Shall we greet our delightful guest?"

He nodded without saying anything to her and they both went down the steps, to the hallway where Everilda was patiently waiting for someone or something to give her some attention. She looked like she had been waiting for a while and when Isra slowly appeared at the bottom of the steps; Everilda grimaced and affixed a fake smile as the witch she had long hated, Lady Isra, looked at her for the first time in years.

Isra agitated the bitter failure of a witch by announcing, "Well if it isn't old Everilda, the failure in all things!"

This caused Everilda to instantly tense up and a bitter sigh came speedily from her lips much to Isra's amusement and joy at seeing the bitter hag defeated in her presence.

12

Isra continued her insult of Everilda, teasing her with the very question the powerless witch did not want to be asked.

"So how is life being mortal? Do tell me! I bet it's frightfully dull!"

Everilda paused and sighed. "Yes, it is frightfully dull indeed, but then you wouldn't know anything about that!" she snapped although she was trying her hardest to be polite.

Isra responded in a sarcastic tone. "Yes, but then again, I never lost my powers by turning my coven leader into a worm!" Resisting a sneaky laugh at the thought of such a thing happening, she then said sarcastically, "I suppose he was so pleased with you after that incident."

Everilda turned away from Isra in an effort to avoid the subject, but Isra had other ideas, and issued yet another blow to poor, ill-fated Everilda. "Well after that, I can't blame the man for taking away your powers. I would imagine there is no way of getting them back either."

Everilda knew this. She knew there was no possible way of getting her powers back and wasn't particularly enjoying being exposed in conversation, but alas she had come to see Isra so it was to be expected from her old foe. Old wounds were bound to be brought up, opening the past with the present, new scars and fresh blood billowing out of those scars that made them seem as fresh as yesterday.

She knew Isra would do so before she even came here. She knew exactly how Isra would respond to her appearance and that she would throw her past mistakes in her face. The question was: why come seek Isra out when she knew she would get only backlash? Was Everilda trying to provoke Lady Isra of the Dark? If so, she was aiming in the wrong direction as Astrid was now the dark force of the tower and even Isra didn't know just how powerful and menacing he had become.

The raven-man stood not too far away from his love watching the two women talk, but under disguise. He wasn't in his raven or human form, but had transmuted himself into simply energy within. He had become actual living energy and he was carefully listening to every word that was spoken between Everilda and Isra.

Astrid had also recently acquired himself a victim in Contessia, the Wiccan girl who had befriended Klinq and was now under the mystic reign of Lady Isra who had made the girl an offer to teach her dark magics. Astrid had magically disarmed Contessia after he created a magical energy attack that hit the entire tower and all its inhabitants.

So poor Contessia was now under Astrid's wicked control. Nobody knew anything about it, and there was no clue as to how she had ended up asleep on the floor in the main room as she did not remember a thing, which was perfect for Astrid's evil plan. He could toy with her mentally whenever he wished and she would be at his mercy, no matter how much she tried not to be.

Contessia had already had her fair share of torture since coming to the tower and being in the midst of Lady Isra and Astrid. Her first night at the tower was a terrifying one where she was woken in the night by a strange noise that hypnotized her and led her to a tunnel of hell.

She had followed the enticing tunnel until she saw an old, rustic door and being the naïve girl she was, she opened it to which she found a staircase surrounded by spiders that covered the stairwell and every possible exit.

Of course, when she tried to run back and exit the tunnel, the door had been magically blocked by three planks of wood and she had no choice but to face the spiders. A horrifying plight she hated having to endure and screamed her way through it until she had ran to safety and banged on the door of Klinq's basement, waking him and reliving her plight as she and the gnome began to understand just how frightening it really was to be in the company of Lady Isra of the Dark.

However, Lady Isra wasn't behind the attack. When Contessia met Astrid in his human form, he found great amusement in her situation and it had given her the idea that he was in fact her attacker—not Isra—and she wasn't wrong.

Astrid was behind it all but Isra was up to her own tricks, befriending Contessia and taking her under her dark wing so she was ultimately being controlled by both of these magnificent beings.

The question to be pondered was: who was more dangerous, Astrid or Isra?

Isra was known as Lady Isra of the Dark and for a good reason; she was dark, she'd taken human lives, and she was a powerful force to be both feared and respected. Astrid, on the other hand, was knowledgeable in magical arts and was also very dark but unlike Isra, he had a bit more humanity in him. However, this did not stop him from committing the foulest of deeds. He was more treacherous in how he approached his wicked endeavors.

Astrid continued to listen as Lady Isra and Everilda were still in deep conversation, mainly insults from Isra to Everilda. He had the distinct impression that Isra was not a fan of Everilda and that she actually enjoyed taunting her old foe.

Everilda was more complacent and trying to get some attention from Isra about her plight which sadly was not working in this instance as Isra was shooting her down every chance she got and why wouldn't she? They were enemies, after all.

Isra found the mortal Everilda amusing in every aspect. She had long been laughing at the witch—or more accurately now, ex-witch—for many years, long before she had ever lost her powers. Everilda was a complete joke to Isra and she had made this clear from the moment Everilda had stepped foot in Isra's home.

It seemed to be more likely that Everilda was seeking something from Isra by traveling all the way to get to the tower as Isra had a lot of power, then Astrid paused as he remembered her grand entrance with the lightning show. How could a mortal put on such a feat with no magic? A mortal that had lost her powers, no less.

It didn't make sense at all. There had to be more here than it appeared to be. There had to be something Everilda wasn't saying. A mortal wouldn't have access to magic but they may know beings in high places that did and that could pose a threat; so why on earth was she here?

He was going to make it his personal mission to find out all he could about Everilda and her intentions. That was a promise, and if he found out something he didn't like, he would deal with it personally and Isra would not be involved; this he had quickly decided without hesitation. If his girl knew things, she could become in danger despite being a powerful, almighty witch. No, he was going to deal with this foul creature himself, he decided, firmly.

The next few days would require a lot of determination and cunning valor in order to find out Everilda's agenda and why she was here seeking friendship or possibly something more sinister from Lady Isra of the Dark.

He was done eavesdropping on their conversation and had decided to lurk in the background as he swiftly changed back into his raven form in the blink of an eye and before anyone could notice, the man had vanished. He was now going to turn his attention back to Contessia who was in the main room of the tower, sitting cross-legged in the dark with some candles placed on the floor next to her.

He watched her closely as she focused on the candles and sprinkled different herbs on them while uttering words and moving her hands, signaling energies to come forth from beyond. She wasn't very experienced in the dark way of things, having been raised by a

Wiccan clan, but she was able to manipulate energy and silvery blue sparks emerged from her fingers.

Astrid took a step back, because even in his raven form he wanted to be unseen to Contessia who seemed to have been taking instruction from Lady Isra very well despite her lack of education in the dark arts. Isra had taken Contessia under her wing to tutor her in magics of the darker variety but knowing Isra, Astrid figured there would be a deeper purpose for this offer of education to the young, spirited Wiccan.

Isra had not yet revealed her intentions toward Contessia, but she could be sweet and kind when she wanted to be; she could also masquerade her evil into something as sweet as pie in appearance. Astrid was doing the same, but nobody knew just how much of his dark and cruel nature was coming out to play in this notorious tower that was already inhabited by one treacherous villain, Lady Isra.

Astrid was giving her a run for her money by enacting more feats of horror, torment, and pain in such a small space of time than Isra had done in her entire life. He was the bad guy in this, in every sense of the word.

Contessia seemed unnerved as she continued to practice magic in the dark room where Astrid was perched on the window ledge, quietly watching her. She was looking paler than usual and her purple hair was fading significantly, which since Astrid had magically disarmed her, suggested to him that she was losing power, not gaining it, which she thought she was.

She didn't have much power to shout about to begin with, but she was a Wiccan at heart, so magic was in her blood and it coursed through her veins as did nature. She was born and had lived in the natural forest wilderness for most of her life in this world.

I doubt her Wiccan clan would be too impressed with her choice now though, taking lessons in the dark arts from Lady Isra of the Dark, a witch who had a notorious reputation for good reason and who was also a killer.

Astrid paused for a moment and flapped his wings loudly, generating a series of sirens that sounded off fantastically loud throughout the small room. One by one, these loud sirens that came out of nowhere went off, getting increasingly louder and more offensive by the second.

Contessia had no idea what was going on while she tried bravely to find the loud shrieking sound; it prickled her intensely so much that she covered her ears in defeat. The noise was too wild for her calm exterior.

Astrid seized his moment to transform back to man and watched the helpless girl fighting the noise to no avail as everything in her world turned grey from inside her eyes. She couldn't see anything, she was almost blind. Her eyes began to feel heavy, and her head felt like jelly and she held onto the wall for support.

She cried out, "Someone, please help me!!"

And the raven-man was more than happy to carry out her request; he quietly placed his hands on the back of her head and suddenly her mind was a chaotic mess. All her emotions flooded, sending her in a catastrophic frenzy as she lost control of her mind and her body.

She couldn't see Astrid behind her, but the damage was done. He had her totally under his willful control. His hands slowly moved from the back of her head down to her neck as he sent the most toxic energy jolts down her spine, disarming her and controlling her body's every move.

She screamed; the pain in her spine was staggering her senses, leaving her unable to get away from Astrid. She couldn't run from the devilish grip he had her under. The torture he was inflicting onto her was getting more and more devastating each time but he wasn't done with Contessia, not yet.

He waited as she attempted to find some fluid motion in her body by trying to move her arms but alas, no luck. She was paralyzed again. She couldn't stand. She couldn't move any of her limbs. She may as well have been turned to stone.

Astrid was doing a marvelous job of torturing the young Contessia. And he knew it. He looked at her proudly from afar as she stood in front of him, unable to move or see him. She was under his ferocious spell.

He looked at her as if she were his best work, as if she were a painting that had been painted stroke by stroke. He admired her pain and he enjoyed her suffering. He paused and pondered about what could come from ripping her spine out of her body while she was still alive. He figured it would hurt and he imagined the pain she would be in.

He closed his eyes to relish the moment as he thought wildly to himself about this fantasy of Contessia in agonizing pain with this latest addition to her torture that he was delivering unto her. He stopped to look at the clock and saw he had been here with Contessia, paralyzing her and sending her body into a vortex of hellish torture for almost a full hour.

He paused and thought of Isra; she would be looking for him and she still had the notorious mortal Everilda in tow, of whom he wanted to monitor closely. Astrid left Contessia in her paralyzed state and then headed down the steps before turning and swiftly signaling his finger to set her free and able to move again, for now. He continued down the steps until he was near the main door that led into the grounds of the tower.

It was just approaching sunrise as he stepped out and his beloved Isra was standing against a tree, watching as the sun slowly appeared in the sky.

He noticed the light was shining on her face as her long white hair cascaded below her shoulders and down her slender frame. She looked somber; her eyes displayed a poignant image as Astrid watched her from a distance. She appeared to be reflecting in quiet solitude.

He admired her from a distance and then he moved closer because his longing for her was too intense and he slowly walked behind her, taking care to be quiet until his face softly brushed against her neck, interrupting her train of thought entirely as she was immersed in his kiss.

13

Isra continued to embrace her man as she whispered, "I wasn't expecting to find you."

He nuzzled her and softly replied, "But I wanted to find you."

This pleased her to know that she was wanted and loved by the raven-man and it gave her great encouragement to know he had missed her so much for the few hours they had been away from each other. It reminded her of how strong the relationship was between her and Astrid and in honest truth, it just made her happy to hear him say it. She held him tightly as he held her even closer to him, wrapping his arms with a firm grip around her waist.

He whispered slowly as he kissed her, "I will always want you."

They could have spent hours in their warm embrace with soft, sensual kisses, but as she looked at him, she realized the sun had fully made its appearance and the day had begun.

"And I will always want you," she answered sweetly. "I need you to be in your raven form for a little while though."

"Why?"

She looked him in the eyes. "Everilda seems to want a war. She has come here looking for something and I can promise she will get it. Not the thing she is seeking, but she will get what she has asked for!"

Astrid realized that Isra was on to Everilda and he didn't need to warn her. She had worked out she was up to something on her own.

He admired her assertiveness and replied, "I am glad, because I don't like or trust that woman Everilda, she seems to be seeking your attention and I don't want them wasted as they could be focused on other things."

She noticed his concern. She loved this, how much he thought of her as well as her well-being and she felt privileged that he showed concern for her

"Oh she is seeking my attention all right, but she is not getting what she wants." She pulled away from him slightly and remarked, "Well, come on. The day is getting ahead of us. Come, we must go."

She was signaling him to turn back into a raven when she said this. She loved him in his human form but she also liked the mystery of him and the intrigue he possessed when he was in his dark feathered disguise. And with a wave of his hand, Astrid transformed from man into the raven again and flew over to Lady Isra's hand to embrace the witch's request.

Lady Isra needed him in his raven form for the moment, as she wanted him to be unseen while she figured out the situation with Everilda and her motives. It would also be a perfect time for Astrid to do his own digging; he was highly intuitive and could read things very well.

Lady Isra was preparing for battle. If Everilda's aim was to fully grasp Isra's attention, she had it and was going to get what she truly deserved.

The mortal or witch as she once was, wasn't staying in Lady Isra's tower as she didn't have an invitation to occupy the premises and Isra made this very clear to Everilda. She had no choice but to seek shelter elsewhere for the duration of her stay. Everilda and Isra made plans to meet again though and Isra was going to use the opportunity to its full potential to analyze Everilda and find out why she was here seeking her out.

I mean, a witch who was no longer a witch and made an immortal, that can't be good news, right? She would have been banished after that.

Isra had her suspicions as did Astrid as to why she was here. Neither she nor Astrid liked or trusted the mortal Everilda and after her lightning show in which she presented herself to Astrid—which Isra did not know about—but who could blame them?

In any case, they would soon find out what she was doing there and why she had come to the home of Lady Isra of the Dark, years after losing her powers and being banished.

Today was quiet; the air signaled a calm energy so she made plans to get out of the tower for the day and go into the forest. She included her beloved companion Astrid who often enjoyed her company when it was just the two of them alone.

He cawed at the thought of it with excitement as she fed him a worm and then prepared a basket ready for the day. His face was excited at the prospect of just him and his witch spending time together in the forest

Isra had decided to venture out today as she felt a need for the fresh air that she didn't get to experience often since she mainly stayed in the safety of her tower. She needed to feel nature's touch on her skin, even if for a short while. It wasn't that she was afraid; she was used to being inside the tower. She was, in many ways, a recluse and didn't interact with anyone except Astrid, but he was perfectly okay with that.

Today would be a good opportunity to reconnect with nature and get a feel for things. She was preparing herself for a war with Everilda and so she wanted to take the time to rejuvenate herself and prepare herself for what was to come.

Everilda was acting as a friend toward Isra, but appearances can be extremely deceiving and Lady Isra was not fooled by the ex-witch's demeanor as she knew there had to be more to it than what was being played out in front of her eyes. Everilda had nothing and so with Isra still being supreme with her magic, it would be fair to assume that Everilda had come seeking out Isra for her magic or perhaps something else. Astrid was suspicious and also concerned but unbeknown to Isra, he was going to do his own digging on the ex-witch, just to make sure Isra was safe. And if the raven-man had any reason to think that Isra was under attack by Everilda, he would deal with her swiftly and efficiently to protect his love.

Isra strode through the trees casually without a care in the world with Astrid flying above close by to the witch, ever faithful. They walked for a good few miles until they were greeted by a place they had not seen before that was secluded and cut off from the rest of the world.

It was strange they had not come across this place, it was as if it had appeared out of nowhere by magic. Isra and Astrid often walked and explored the areas and knew most of them; finding a new place was mesmerizing and also intriguing.

Isra felt the energies of this strange place with her hands as she took in the sights around her. Trees stood mighty and tall, lush and green with fruits dangling down from every branch. They invited her to explore them further as they looked so tantalizing to the senses. Flowers vastly decorated the area in vibrant shades of pink, yellow, orange, purple and green, all bright with nature's most dedicated helpers in the form of honeybees, ladybirds, and butterflies that fluttered softly between each flower.

It was like something out of another world and then, out of the corner of her eye, she saw something small yet shiny with glistening wings. It couldn't be … but no, she wasn't seeing things. There were fairies here! It was mesmerizing to the witch. She had long wanted to see fairies again, having not seen one since she was a child.

She sat quietly on the grass next to a pink rose and watched silently as they fluttered around her, their wings glittering in the shadows as she watched wonderment. She was thrilled and happy to be able to see such a fantastical and magical sight. Astrid didn't have much care for fairies and instead sat next to his love and watched fondly as her eyes fixated on the fairy folk.

Her gaze was fully fixed on them, and it was interesting for him to see as he knew she had no fondness for humans; animals and magical creatures were a much different thing. She did have love inside her heart as black as it was, and this picturesque scene had now confirmed that fact to Astrid. This wonderful place was magical and yet enchanting to all who saw it, but Astrid had his suspicions as Isra was very much enchanted by it all, as she was by all magical things.

He was cautious and wondered why they had never encountered it before ... and why was it so vivid and colorful in nature and so captivating to Lady Isra?

He was suspicious but didn't say anything to his witch as he didn't want to break her enchanted and lifted spirit that was very much lifted in this moment. Isra was captivated by the sights, she was enthralled by the beauty around her but she did love the nature and fantasy of magic. She always had been. It was in her. She lived in darkness but the true nature of magic was something she admired with a fond passion as it came directly from the heart.

I'm not saying she hated being dark because she loved being dark, but true magical elements like this really caught her attention and kept her distracted; that was the part that worried Astrid.

Isra and Astrid had been at this wonderful location for what seemed like many hours, she had slowly watched the fairies as they went about their business and attended to the flowers and she had walked around smelling the flowers and admired the beauty and serenity of this place. She looked longingly at one of the apple trees and was about to reach for one when something caught her eye and her ears, all at once.

She didn't know what it was but a sound was heard and she saw something in the corner of her eye. It made her eyes dart everywhere at once; she could do this of course. Being so gifted in the magical arts, her eyes could dart from side to side very fast in order to spot something that had caught her attention.

She had put her hand out, ready to reach for the apple while her eyes still darted everywhere around her as she was surveying the situation and the strange occurrence that had her listening and looking keenly. It wasn't making a lot of noise, but she knew something was there, something in the background that you sense and also see, if you get my meaning.

She was now on red alert. Her hand had dropped down and was feeling the energy from this strange thing that had her mind on overdrive. She wasn't crazy but she was in tune with what was around her at this very moment.

The paradise land she had found herself in was a bit of a mystery as they had never found this place before despite many walks around the forest when Lady Isra and Astrid explored the land together. It was bizarre and it could easily be deemed that the land had appeared overnight with a wave of a magic wand, designed and structured in a flash.

Isra, being a witch, knew from experience that colorful and beautifully tempting things are put in front of someone in order to distract them and knock them off course but she wasn't knocked of course so easily but the thought had transfigured in her mind of what this could be.

She wasn't stupid and she sure as hell wasn't dumb. Yes, the magnificent beauty of the place had indeed captivated her soul and enchanted her but she was aware that something was amiss. She opened her eyes and turned around to see that the apple tree that once stood behind her totally disappeared; it was gone without a trace.

Strange, she pondered, but questioned its nonexistence that was apparent all of a sudden.

Why would it disappear?

What had caused it to disappear?

She turned to Astrid and paused thoughtfully. "We should leave this place and go home. There is something not right here."

Astrid followed his lover's move and also checked out the area carefully, sensing the energies that were around him. He felt it too. He couldn't work out what it was but something was there, watching both him and Isra, right then.

"We are being watched!" he muttered quietly under his breath but he made sure it was loud enough for Isra to hear.

She responded calmly as her eyes advanced as she did so. "Yes, that is apparent, but why?"

Isra looked at the flowers; they were still vibrant and bright as ever and she wondered what could animate them to be so captivating to the eye. The apple tree was gone, she was aware of that too, but everything else that showed the beauty of this place was still here, the flowers, and the fairies she had seen not long ago, all of it was still here.

It caused her to think hard. Why remove the apple tree and leave everything else still here? What was indeed so precious and unique about the apple tree that it had to disappear? Was it enchanted?

She stopped herself in mid flow as she realized she already knew the answer to that question: of course it was enchanted. The whole place was enchanted; the entire location she was standing in was a product of magic. She *knew* that.

She sat down on a log and pointed herself and her feet directly at the ground only to find she was in front of a stream and this too was enchanting. The water told her this notion vibrantly as it glittered with many shades of blue that sparkled with many tranquil feelings as she gently immersed her hands in the stream and felt it for the first time.

It wasn't pure, but yet she found no harm from touching the water. She wisely decided against drinking it, by better judgment as she knew temptation could lurk in all forms. She paused and stayed silent for a moment and then summoned Astrid without saying a word as he instantly flew over to the log and appeared at her side.

She smiled but firmly asserted to him, "I think this is something to do with Everilda. I'm not too sure, but we can never be too certain on these things."

He nodded his raven head and agreed. "Yes, I believe it is too, but I am glad you are not fooled by this magical fantasy as I know you are fond of the idealism of fantasy and magic in its truest form."

He did not want to hurt her feelings with the truth he had just spoken. He joined her in silence as he thought and then as it was if he had a new idea in his mind. He inquired, "If this is the work of

Everilda, how is she managing it without magic? She is a mortal, is she not?"

Lady Isra turned to her faithful friend and smiled as she answered him with an inquisitive look on her face that told him she was not surprised. "Yes, she is, but she may have hired help. Mortals cannot do things like this alone. There must be someone she has helping her."

"We must find out whom," he said instantaneously, remembering he was already planning to do his own research on Everilda without Isra's knowledge.

She stood up, picking up her basket and preparing to leave and replied, "Well, I can only trust you with that duty."

"I know," he said smiling and then settled on Isra's lap and stretched his wings and then asked, "So are you planning on meeting Everilda soon? In order to gather more knowledge on her?"

Isra answered him softly. "Yes my friend, and it may just be another beautiful day of learning ahead. But not so beautiful for Everilda."

She found herself amused by the concept as Everilda was not beautiful.

14

Isra and Astrid walked the long trudge, many miles back to the tower after their brief but intriguing visit in the magical land they'd discovered.

They'd got home just as the sun was setting and the sky was covered in dark clouds, but they were surprised to find that Contessia was not there. Isra was more surprised than Astrid at Contessia not being there. She had expected to be graced with her presence this evening and this would now cause her plans to be changed.

Isra came into the main sitting room to find a note Contessia had left on the window sill. The note was hastily written, as if it was done in a hurry and it read:

Hello Isra, I had to meet a friend, terribly sorry to let you down but this was urgent. See you soon, Contessia.

Isra folded the note up and discarded it out of the window as she turned to Astrid and remarked, "Well, this is just convenient, isn't it? I wonder what could have occurred to make our Contessia feel the need to vacate at such short notice."

The raven shook his head in response. "Perhaps something presented itself to her in a way of an opportunity to socialize," he suggested.

Isra laughed as she pondered that notion; as far as she was aware, Contessia didn't have anyone besides her Wiccan clan, who she guessed wouldn't be too impressed at Contessia for learning the dark arts with a witch as notorious as herself.

Also, her alliance with Klinq had broken down since the cowardly gnome refused to stand up for the girl following a series of attacks that had been bestowed upon her since her arrival in the tower.

Isra remarked sharply without thinking, "The silly girl doesn't have anyone to socialize with and I can bet that since she has been here, this is even truer now than it was before!"

Astrid also laughed, remembering that he had been socializing with Contessia in a snide and devious way but the poor girl had no clue that her attacker, who had been playing these great feats of torture on her, was him because she had been paralyzed every single time. To Astrid, she was like a toy that a bored child would get out of the box every so often to amuse themselves with.

He contained his amusement as Isra did not know what he had been doing with Contessia. It wasn't as if he had been betraying her, his heart always stayed loyal to Isra, but to him, Contessia was just a fun way to pass the time.

He thought about what might happen if Isra had found out about his wicked antics with the young Wiccan girl and he wondered if his witch would be mad with him. He hoped she wouldn't but in the same train of thought, he feared that she might get angry with him because he had kept it from her.

Actually, he had kept a few things from her but only because he was worried she might get upset or resent him and in turn reject him if she knew, so out of his love and not wanting to lose her, he had simply not told her everything.

Of course the torture he was inflicting upon Contessia was something he was enjoying very much and he wasn't sure at this point whether Isra would understand his reasoning for it. He was like her, dark, but his darkness was a little better hidden than hers. He could be tight-lipped about things about himself as he was very private. He wasn't the type to go about shouting his business in the public view; he was more restrained than that. He also had integrity in himself that he was respected for greatly among those he had grown up with and those who had come to know him.

Unlike Isra, Astrid had control over his anger and didn't do things on impulse. He was a lot calmer and his emotions were much more balanced but again, he never mentioned these things to his love as he didn't want to offend the witch by bringing her imperfections to the light.

He kept his amusement safely contained inside himself as he replied, "Yes, my love, that is true; the girl does not have many friends outside of us, but are we *really* her friends?"

Isra smiled and then paused. "Probably not in the way she thinks."

She then had a sudden thought about Klinq; she hadn't seen the gnome for a while and something made her want to question him. Astrid watched with great intrigue as his witch fled down the stairs in a hurry, making her way down to the basement where Klinq dwelled. He followed her immediately to find out just why she wanted to seek him out, now.

To her surprise, the basement was empty, Klinq was gone, his clothes were gone and even his old, moldy pile of books he had positioned on the shelf were gone too. It was not clear when he had vacated but it was clear he had wanted his move to be kept secret.

"That filthy gnome. Such a coward! He's gone!" she uttered amid a torrent of rage. "He better not have betrayed me!" she said sharply.

Astrid seized this opportunity to transform back into his human form. It was quick and his wings soon became arms and grabbed his beloved from behind while whispering into her ear, "Don't worry about him. He is no longer our problem."

"I guess not." She sighed and then added, "I do wonder why he suddenly felt the need to leave."

Astrid had a sudden thought come to him. With the previous plans Isra had with Contessia now disrupted, he could go out and do some digging on Everilda. He had decided it was in Isra's best interests for her to not know about his plans at this time.

He turned to his witch and remarked, "I think I will head out for a little while. I feel up to a worm or two. I will be back in a few hours."

Lady Isra nodded acknowledging his words. "Hmmm that is a thought. I think you should go and seek out our Klinq on your travels, make sure he has been behaving himself," she said sweetly as Astrid realized that she wanted him to spy on Klinq.

Of course, he had no problem with this as it fit in with his dynamic scheme greatly. Astrid flew off in a hurry as Lady Isra watched him go, watching his feathers behind him as he disappeared into the morning sky. He scoured the skies vigorously looking for his two targets, first Klinq, as he wanted that one out of the way, and then Everilda which was his prime target.

His excuse about seeking out worms had been a feeble one, but he trusted in himself that what he was doing was right. He didn't need to worry Isra until he found something worth telling, for he knew the witch would worry and so he simply didn't feel the need to activate that in her.

Klinq was soon spotted heading toward Spindlevitch by the raven Astrid's beady eyes and he could see the gnome was in a hurry. He stopped in mid-flight, watching Klinq in deep conversation with someone. Astrid perched on a tree branch as he watched the gnome talking to the mysterious being and it was no surprise when he saw the famous red and black cloak. It was Everilda.

Oh my, two birds with one stone, he thought to himself quickly.

Everilda looked incredibly impatient as she pressed the gnome for information.

"So what did you find?" she asked him quizzically.

"Lady Isra and Astrid are both intrigued by your appearance but they are not easily fooled and are suspicious, dear mistress!" he said quickly as Everilda tapped her foot on the floor.

"Ah yes, Astrid; he seems to be quite the protective figure to Isra. If only there was some way of eradicating him..." Everilda remarked sarcastically.

She felt defeated by Astrid's presence in Lady Isra's life. She would love to get rid of the raven but she knew such things would not be possible or feasible.

Klinq continued on, rambling as he did so. "But it doesn't matter now, mistress, for I have left my duties. I have lost a good friend due to this mess and I do not wish to be involved any further in this fiasco between you and the witch. Sorry, the more powerful witch," he added just a little too firmly, he realized after he had said it.

Everilda snapped her fingers. "How dare you leave! I put you in that tower and only I can say when you may leave. You are a disgrace to magics of all forms, Sir Klinq."

She snapped again as she pointed a finger toward him. She was furious but the gnome was in no danger. Astrid now knew everything he needed to know. Klinq was aligned with Everilda and Klinq's appearance at their residence was instigated by Everilda in a weak attempt to learn more about Isra.

Klinq had left the tower of Lady Isra of the Dark because he didn't want to be a spy any longer and so Astrid knew he wasn't a threat, just a stupid coward who had not only pissed off one witch, but three. As he had lost his friend Contessia too, who had seen him for what he was, a coward who couldn't stand up for her.

"Oh dear, he has got himself into quite a sticky mess," Astrid remarked quietly to himself.

He decided he would leave Klinq to it. Someone like that didn't need much help in making a situation worse, for Astrid knew Klinq would do that all by himself. Astrid had watched Everilda and Klinq for long enough and now it was time to report back to Isra and tell her of what he had learnt on his travels.

Everilda huffed in defeat, pacing the stone floor as she realized her plans were coming apart at the seams and she needed something to try and rectify that. Befriending Isra hadn't worked, for the witch knew Everilda was up to no good and she wasn't easily fooled. Then when she had created the mystic land to try leading Isra astray with her love for magic that had also failed her because the witch knew in her intuition that although it was beautiful, it wasn't real.

Everilda thought furiously as she knew she was running out of ideas to get to Isra. She would have to be more cunning, cleverer; but what could she do to get back at the witch for making her lose her powers? Most of the options had already been explored. Lady Isra wasn't falling for it and quite rightly so; she had great intelligence and she knew that Everilda wasn't here for friendship and sweet kisses.

Everilda sat in her uncomfortable, hard chair positioned next to the stone fireplace and placed her hand on the walls, as she felt the cold chill. She had no money and no power, so an abandoned dungeon was all she could manage for a dwelling. She was disappointed but she was trying not to feel defeated but trying to defeat Isra was already proving to be a defeat of its very own.

She looked to the flames for answers in hope they would come on a winged horse to give her powers back, but no such luck. What could she do?

There must be something, she thought. *There must be some way to get at Isra and infiltrate her operation.*

It was testing her greatly and she wanted to get back at the witch and make her pay but nothing she was doing had worked yet. She needed more time to think on this, but thinking was something Everilda lacked. Everilda suddenly had an idea that sparked like a light bulb in her mind.

Oh, this could work, she thought wickedly. *It could indeed work.*

15

Everilda made haste and journeyed to the center of the forest where Contessia had partaken in rituals with her Wiccan clan. Of course, since she had joined forces with Lady Isra, her presence with her clan had lessened as they feared for her, but nevertheless, Everilda was hoping for the best.

She watched as the Wiccans paraded themselves around their soft flowing tents in a joyous fashion. She watched them, fascinated, as they continued their normal way of life. She couldn't spot Contessia but she did spot an elderly woman talking to some younger Wiccans. Everilda clearly saw this as an opportunity to gather information on Contessia, so she walked over to the woman, letting her cloak drag behind her.

The elder woman looked puzzled as Everilda made her approach, she could see this was a woman who had once been of power but now seemed desperate and futile in her efforts. Desperation was written all over her face. She questioned Everilda as she glanced at the desperate woman of whom she had just met.

"What do you want here? You know this is a place of peace and enlightenment."

She spoke slowly while mixing some ingredients together in a cauldron and then poured a mystery powder over the entire conundrum.

Everilda lowered her voice and said, "Yes, I know, but I have business with one of your own. She's young with long purple hair and is a sweet thing for a witch. If she *is* one," she added sarcastically.

The woman, also known as Agnes to her clan, knew exactly who Everilda was referring to and she didn't hold back as she sternly replied, "I know who you have business with and she is protected here despite her silly behavior and ideas over the recent months."

Agnes was referring to Contessia joining the ranks of Lady Isra; the woman clearly thought Contessia was playing with fire as she explained this notion to Everilda who wasn't put off by the elderly woman's warning.

"Well, that is something I will risk as I have business with this young lady! She is interesting to me for a purpose! She may well be Lady Isra's undoing and that excites me greatly," Everilda finished sweetly, hoping this part would change Agnes' mind.

Agnes paused as she heard this. "If that is the case, it could be good for all of us! The one you seek often walks into the forest in the mornings but be careful, for she is powerful despite her poorly thought-out decisions," she uttered solemnly.

"Thank you, that is where I shall be heading next!" Everilda muttered decisively.

Agnes nodded and added, "She is seldom here these days. Her new life with Lady Isra has taken precedence over everything else, but I hope she is wise enough to learn from this experience and regain her light."

Everilda smiled at the woman as she walked away. It would be very easy now to get a meeting with Contessia.

Night fall was approaching by the time Everilda reached the forest where she was told she could find Contessia. Everilda slowly scanned the area for signs of the purple haired girl. She knew Contessia was naïve and could easily be lured, but the trouble would be how to spot her.

Her purple hair would make her stand out in even the greenest of forests such as this one, so that was a good place to start. But Everilda wanted to seek the girl out magically. However, that would be tremendously difficult with no magic or powers to speak of, so she would have to be more original in her approach.

The purple haired girl wasn't very difficult to find. Contessia was gathering flowers meticulously as she arranged them in their respective colors; white and lilac. Everilda saw Contessia in her serene manner and made haste in making her approach as she watched Contessia's purple hair contrast with the rays of the sun as though her hair emitted brilliant lights across the sky. The Wiccan girl was clearly in a state of natural bliss, feeling at home in the floral wilderness, not noticing that Everilda was almost in her physical presence.

The former witch tapped Contessia on the shoulder which startled the girl. She exclaimed, "Oh my, who are *you*? I am forbidden to speak to strangers, especially those who don't follow the old ways."

Everilda lowered herself in a graceful fashion and spoke slowly. "Don't be cautious, dear, I am simply an old woman looking to make your acquaintance. My name is Edith and I come to you for answers on a very old problem I have," she finished, hoping that she had Contessia's full attention.

Contessia looked at Everilda, now known as Edith, and remarked, "Oh, well I'm just a witch in training really, so I do not know if I can help you."

Contessia was lying; she was in training, but she was more than confident in her abilities. It was something about Edith that unnerved her and after everything she had been through since her alliance with Lady Isra; the young witch was going to be very cautious.

She studied Edith closely, starting with her shoulder length fair hair. She had also noticed that red presented itself on the woman's cloak; this was a woman of passion and anger and maybe even jealousy, Contessia surmised to herself as she looked back at the woman who was asking for her assistance.

Contessia was wary but she didn't know how to get herself out of a situation like this, Lady Isra was back at the tower and Contessia wasn't sure if Isra would help her anyway. Contessia didn't even know if Isra liked her or not, and that in itself was a conundrum.

She had no choice but to accept her fate and speak to her newfound acquaintance, who was staring back at her while also smiling. A clear sign of danger, especially when Everilda was smiling! But Contessia was not wise enough about these things to know better.

"But I could try! What is it you need?" she asked Edith.

Everilda cleared her throat before she spoke. "I hear you are a woman of great connections. You know someone I knew in the past and I am trying to make her acquaintance again but alas, she will not have me as her companion and I am so desperately trying to help her despite her lack of perception."

Everilda paused and then continued softly. "She is a dark soul, although she now believes she has love as well as her power, but I fear it is not to be. I wish to keep an eye on her to simply keep her safe because I fear great heartbreak is to be bestowed upon her."

She was quite astonished at the performance that came from her mouth and put her hand over her mouth to stop herself from laughing.

Contessia became puzzled and had an inkling that Edith was talking about Lady Isra but she needed confirmation from her new friend so she questioned wildly, "What is your friend's name?"

Everilda spoke even slower now as she replied, "Isra."

Contessia was right, Edith was seeking out the one she had recently started an alliance with, but what would this mean for her?

Why ask her of all the folk that she could have asked? Surely her new friend could simply ask someone else to help her with this intimidating task. These questions all formed inside Contessia's mind as she pondered them and their meaning.

Contessia narrowed her eyes in suspicion as Everilda continued on with her speech. "Isra and I have not spoken for many years and although I have tried a recent reconciliation, I believe she doubts my intentions," Everilda uttered quickly as she knew most of that was true.

Contessia's and Everilda's eyes met for a moment as Everilda locked Contessia in a deep and mesmerizing trance. She had the young Wiccan's gaze locked inside hers, and now she wanted to get inside Contessia's head for the best possible results.

Everilda wasn't just going for Isra, she wanted to take her power too and Contessia would be an easy pathway to both! Getting inside Isra's inner circle was her goal but the thing that Everilda didn't know was that Contessia and Isra weren't at all close, but at this moment in time she thought her plan was going from strength to strength and so that small detail had slipped her mind.

Contessia's eyes turned a deep shade of violet as she felt the bewitching charm of Everilda's curse. She began to feel dizzy as the trance got more intense with each heartbeat, making her sweat as her heart pounded faster and faster with each exhilarating breath. Everything Contessia thought she knew would be different as Everilda had a fine handle on the young witch's mind and was slowly changing all the things she wanted Contessia to forget.

She had removed the memory of her and Contessia meeting so that if questioned, the young Wiccan would not be able to recall it. She also manipulated events in Contessia's head so that she would see things very differently as opposed to how they really were. Contessia, who was still in the deep trance, was motionless as she stood before Everilda. She even waved a finger in front of Contessia's face without reaction!

Everilda stood back, admiringly looking at Contessia as she announced, "And now you, dear Contessia, shall be my slave. Anything you hear about or from Lady Isra, you shall report back to me! So shall it be!"

Everilda snapped her fingers and Contessia's eyes opened at once, as if she had finally awakened from a deep, enchanting slumber. And with that, it was done. Contessia was now going to tell Everilda everything she wanted to know and she would have no notion as to why.

However, the question remained: how had Everilda managed to control Contessia when she had no powers? Had she borrowed power from someone else?

Whatever it was, it could only mean one thing. Things were heating up and soon Isra and Everilda would be in a fierce battle, going head-to-head, all in the name of power. Everilda still believed that it would be her that would win out in these festivities between herself and Lady Isra of the Dark.

Yes, she was overly confident and having a new spy in the form of Contessia just made her even more confident because now she had a worthy accessory, a pawn to use however she felt necessary.

Contessia was now Everilda's ammunition to use in this deep heated combat between herself and Lady Isra.

Woes betide for Everilda if Isra suspected anything was amiss, because surely that would mean Everilda's head was going to roll!

16

When Contessia arrived back at the tower that evening, she was quiet and distant, not the usual bubbly, smiling girl that had a magical and positive outlook on everything.

Astrid was the first to notice her change in behavior and remarked, "Contessia, why so glum? You don't seem like yourself tonight."

Isra narrowed her eyes carefully at Contessia, noticing the Wiccan girl was different in her demeanor than usual.

Contessia dropped her fork and said slowly, "I am not too sure. Why, I feel in a daze! I cannot fathom it but it is like something has struck me sorely!"

She touched her forehead anxiously. She felt strange and sore, but had no clue as to why. Maybe she was losing her mind. She didn't know what was causing the affliction.

Isra, having watched the young girl talk, chided, "Hmm, I bet I know what the cause of this mysterious infection is!"

Isra looked carefully into Contessia's eyes and noticed they were not as bright. She paid careful attention to bring herself to Contessia's level and she seated herself on the floor in front of the girl and watched her closely. She felt Contessia's forehead as Astrid watched his witch in amazement. She actually seemed to care about the well-being of Contessia.

He was proud and also shocked; he didn't know what to say. He didn't expect this, not from Isra. It was unlike her but maybe something in her was different, but just like what had happened to Contessia, he couldn't fathom what!

Isra closed her eyes for a moment and then removed her hand from Contessia, her eyes closely watching the girl as she continued to survey her condition. She then stood up, keeping strong sight of Contessia,

"You are to stay right where you are, my dear. No more forest adventures for you! Not until we investigate the nature and the cause of your affliction."

Astrid—still in awe of his beautiful and also kind witch—was deeply mesmerized by the moment and imagined what Isra would be like in the presence of other humans. He thought she hated them. He let his imagination run wild as he thought of nothing but Isra in her kind and true to nature state, like he had just now witnessed. He was caught unawares as she appeared next to him, planting a soft, sweet kiss on his forehead. Noticing his distraction, she giggled slightly as he realized he had been daydreaming about her.

Isra turned to face Astrid and announced, "Keep watch on our dear Contessia, my love. I am going out to see what perplexing visions I may find in my midst."

Contessia tried to protest. "Isra, I am fine. You do not have to worry yourself over me!"

Astrid nodded in agreement with his love. "I agree with Isra; something is amiss and we need to find out what! You will stay here under my protection. No arguments!" he insisted firmly.

The raven-man was not one to fight against when it came to him insisting upon something so Contessia had no choice but to stay with him while Isra went about on her travels. She had her reservations about being left alone with Astrid but Contessia trusted and hoped that Isra wouldn't be away for too long as something about the raven-man unnerved her. Still, she couldn't put her finger on just what.

Isra swiftly disappeared up the stairs and returned, adorned in a midnight blue cloak with black detailing that complimented her loose, long black curls perfectly with her piercing green eyes that glowed fiercely in the night. She approached Astrid before leaving and allowed him to bestow upon her a passionate kiss to which he was more than happy to oblige before she disappeared into the night.

Isra headed directly into the clearing of the forest where she and Astrid would usually walk on their many adventures, however this time, something told her to do something different. It was like an inner voice in her ear saying, "Time for a change, Lady Isra of the Dark. Time to use that wild power and make haste in finding your enemy."

Wild power?! She laughed at that part. Yes, she had power, yes she knew how to wield it, but she never believed it was wild. It was just in her and she knew exactly what to do with it and how it would be best incorporated to guarantee the greatest of success!

And find her enemy—Everilda the deceitful—she would indeed do. It wouldn't be hard. Everilda was mortal now, after all, and as far as Isra could clarify, she had no magic to speak of which made her chances of defeating Everilda that much greater than it would be if she was a witch. Isra tuned in to the energies of the forest as she closed her eyes, visually tracking signs of Everilda's physical presence wherever that may be, here or anywhere.

No, she wasn't intending to locate Everilda and make her appear before her; right now, she wanted to metaphysically track Everilda's movements and locate her visually, inside Everilda's mind, the one place a human being could not hide from a witch, in any way, shape or form!

It didn't take long for a trail of images to form inside Isra's mind, showing Everilda in a variety of locations and showing her face clearly so Isra knew it was her. She could see Everilda clearly, standing inside her cold and run-down dungeon facing a painted mural on the wall, looking solemn.

Oh boy, she must be having some real bad times to be living in a place like this, Isra thought as she chuckled to herself with glee.

It was at this moment that Isra longed to see Everilda; she wanted to see her ideas and her mastermind of trickery fail as it slapped her in the face. She wanted to see her, to greatly confront her. It was the small hours of the night now and Isra was busily thinking of how she could see her nemesis face to face.

She went deeper into the forest as she thought of Everilda and her face; she visualized it clearly, focusing on Everilda's dry lips and her tired, weary eyes. She kept this poignant image in her mind as she went deeper and deeper into the parts of the forest where only creatures of the dark could enter.

Isra quietly positioned herself behind a large Yew tree and waited, taking care to place a convenient ray of invisibility over herself that resulted in yellow rays, forming around her head and body as she kept her position in this place of hiding. It didn't take long before she heard voices. She kept listening and pressed her ear close to the trunk of the tree.

There was a male voice and a female voice, although she strongly sensed that these two voices were not coming from a fighting couple that had failed to serenade each other with the sweet songs of love. She was being humorous in her manner, but she knew what she sensed was true; this was not a couple of lovers fighting.

Isra continued to listen as the voices became clearer while she also found the ability to identify the nature of their confrontation. The male voice was timid and spoke to his confronter with extreme caution, fearing her fiery reaction, which she imagined was coming at any moment now. The female was blunt and fierce as she spoke with every word echoing with its wrath and fury as it emitted from her lips.

He trembled in her presence. She brought on his ever-growing fear as she realized what a big impact she was making on his anxiety as he fumbled around, looking for a suitable reason to leave her presence. Isra continued listening from her safely hidden position as the pair argued.

"Well Sir Klinq, yet again you've outdone yourself as the biggest coward and idiot the earth has ever known!!!" she yelled fiercely. Isra heard the male back away one or two steps.

"But if you please, I cannot do what you ask any longer. I have tried and now I learn that you are using my dear friend in the cause of your evil deeds!"

She was cold and callous and just her mere presence unnerved him to the point, he could feel his blood run cold. She mocked him as she replied, "Your *friend* is merely a pawn in the grand scheme of things between the witch and I."

The male replied defensively, "A pawn, how lovely! But you didn't have to use my friend to do your dirty work in spying on the witch and woes betide you if the raven becomes knowledgeable about this. He scares me more than she does!"

The female sourly remarked while laughing, "Oh Sir Klinq, everyone scares you! I bet you are even scared of your own shadow!"

It was at this moment Isra realized these two conversationalists were Everilda and Klinq, but now she possessed the knowledge that he was a spy, sent personally by Everilda in order to gain intelligence about Isra so that she could infiltrate and take her powers from her, making them her own. Isra now knew she had to take great action in the fight against Everilda in order to send her plans of power and glory into a dramatic halt. She continued to listen to the ramblings of Everilda that were being directed at the cowardly gnome's direction.

"You must understand dear, that your friend is someone I need in order to get close to Isra; she is in their warm but yet dark fold, although it makes me want to throw up but it makes her useful to this cause! And I cannot win unless I have a worthy weapon worth wielding, so your 'friend' as you affectionately call her is EXACTLY what I will be using here!!"

Klinq was still feeling defensive and also guilty of how he'd never stood up for Contessia, his dear friend. "Contessia has done nothing wrong to you! Please leave her out of this mess between you and Isra! She is innocent!" Klinq pleaded as he realized his stance wouldn't change Everilda's mind.

He was right as she barked, "No chance in Hell! She is close to the witch and she is going to tell me all I need to know to get Isra's powers and that is the last time I want to hear about it and it is also the last time I EVER want to see you in my presence!!"

Isra stayed silent behind the tree, placing her hands at the bottom of its roots, and she began to gather energy from inside of herself. It was not black; small shiny white sparks emitted from her fingers as she concentrated, visualizing Contessia in a protective bubble. She closed her eyes and found Contessia in the tower, placing her inside the bubble from her position at the tree.

Back at the tower, Astrid was watching as Contessia was suddenly enveloped in the white energy as it formed into a bubble. He smiled as he knew it was his witch. He also knew she was doing something that came from the light. Now, he didn't know what to make of this, however he was proud of her and his smile revealed all she needed to know.

Isra giggled. She saw his sweet smile inside her magical vision and gazed into his eyes for a few moments, and then she opened her eyes again and smiled to herself, for she had achieved a lot in that very moment, although she didn't want to admit this, not just yet! Isra thought about healing Contessia for a minute; okay, so she didn't really like the girl or any human that much, but right now she felt that protecting Contessia was going to be a necessary task in this battle.

She strongly knew in her heart that Everilda would stop at nothing to get what she had, so she had to do whatever it would take to eliminate Everilda from the human and magical realms for good! And that was just what Lady Isra was going to do: Eliminate Everilda, once and for all!

17

Isra waited until Klinq and Everilda had gone their separate ways and then proceeded to make the long journey home. She had learnt many things from their conversation ... or maybe it was more accurate to call it a confrontation!

Isra was shocked to learn that Contessia was implicated in Everilda and Klinq's dirty plot as well, but she should have known better than to trust a gnome as it turned out Klinq was Everilda's spy from day one. His presence in the tower grounds had not been an accident.

However, after witnessing Klinq telling Everilda to leave Contessia out of her plans, Isra knew he had been bullied into it, so she saw him as more of an innocent but yet cowardly third party that had been dragged into a vendetta against his will.

After all, Isra knew Everilda from their time before. They weren't ever friends but back when they were both members of the same coven, Everilda had made a very foolish mistake and accidentally turned the coven leader into a worm. Thinking about this, Isra laughed because she was reminded of how stupid Everilda looked at the time and she became even more amused because Everilda still looked pretty stupid now as a mortal.

Oh, how it brought tears of laughter to her eyes. Isra had to take a minute to compose herself and stopped to wipe her eyes. She was deeply amused by the situation of Everilda and it was even more amusing that in Everilda's warped mind, she thought she could actually defeat Isra. Isra stood back as she thought of this and she truly didn't know whether to laugh or cry at this particular hallucination! It was just so painfully amusing!

She carried on walking the long journey home, as she couldn't wait to get home and tell her dear one, Astrid, all she had found out on her travels.

It was just as the sun was making its appearance to herald the day when she became distracted by something. She wasn't able to ascertain what when suddenly something grabbed her from behind. She immediately acted in self-defense and subconsciously, in her mind, made haste to disarm her attacker, who seemed to find this funny and endearing as they planted a kiss on her.

Isra wasn't used to being kissed by strangers so when she whizzed around to face the attacker, she was pleasantly surprised to be greeted by Astrid's smiling and also very entertained face.

"Well, it's fantastic to know that you don't want my kiss," he joked while cradling her hair in his hands.

"I didn't know it was you! Silly man, although next time I will disarm you!" she replied endearingly while being smothered with his many kisses.

"Oh really?! I look forward to seeing you do that!" he replied, clearly fascinated and enjoying this moment they were having together in the early morning sun.

She got the feeling that he wanted her to disarm him. Oh, he was a cheeky and flirty one, all right. He certainly was flirtatious and she loved his energy. He was passionate and energetic and it made her feel alive, it made her feel more powerful and mighty then she could ever feel. Astrid had that ability to make her feel like the most important person in the world and he was damn good at it too! She sometimes wondered if she was under his spell but he had told her many times when they had met that he wasn't a witch and that he didn't perform magic.

Of course, since being with Isra, he had performed magic and he was exceptionally gifted with the art of magic which she admired and was quite proud of in a sentimental and also loving way.

He suddenly pulled her very close to him, not quite whispering but loud enough for Isra to hear as he said, "I saw you with Contessia. I saw the light in your heart!"

He pointed at her heart with his finger as she looked back at him, not knowing what to say. She was silent but she wasn't running away. She knew he was right, she knew there was warmth and light inside her soul again.

She didn't fully understand it, but she knew that deep down under all that darkness, she did have a good heart or maybe the darkness was now melting away and all that would be left was light. She didn't know but she knew he was seeing right inside her heart. He placed his hand on her heart as he continued with his quest, softly probing the nature of her not so dark heart.

"Where has all this love and deep feeling come from?" he questioned her softly.

She began to speak softly while feeling his hand on her heart with her own. "I truly do not know. I am not used to feeling things like this."

Astrid grabbed her hand with his own and placed it on his chest as he embraced her. "Whatever it is, I like it!"

She stiffened a little. Not by him, not by what he was doing or saying, but she did have more pressing things on her mind. Such as the latest revelation in the course of the Everilda debacle and what she had learned on her secret mission in the forest! She reached for his hand and stopped him mid-embrace as she looked him seriously in the eye. He noticed her strong and yet firm gaze and paid close attention as the words slowly found their way out of her mouth.

"While I was on that reconnaissance mission to find out the cause of Contessia's affliction, I found out something and I'm not sure you're going to like it."

"Oh? And what is that?" he questioned although unbeknown to Lady Isra, he already knew what she was about to validate for him.

"I caught sight of Everilda in the forest as it was very late into the dark of night," she began to explain. "I realized she wasn't alone and her companion was none other than Klinq! They were having a good old skirmish, shouting at each other; well, Everilda was doing the shouting parts and it became clear in the middle of the conversation that Everilda had instructed Klinq to spy on us, more accurately *me*, in order to gain intelligence so that she could attempt to conquer me!"

She continued discerningly, "Of course, like all other things she has strived to succeed in, you and I both know she will fail to conquer me but she has strong ambitions and also believes my power is attainable to her!"

Astrid listened carefully. He had already possessed this knowledge about Everilda but hearing the confidence from his love that she believed Everilda's plan would fail brought much gratification to his soul. He smiled, for he knew in his heart that Isra could defeat Everilda and he knew this was a powerful array of vengeance combined with resentment and bitter rage that had emerged from the past.

He, however, also knowingly had the knowledge that Isra would not lose sight of the real reason behind this and that it would not deter her from the battle. In fact, Astrid knew more about his witch than she claimed to know about herself.

The sun's warming and enlightening rays shined on them both softly as they still stood, wrapped in a deep embrace. The morning was just beginning and they felt the sensuous energies as they slowly unpeeled their lips and hands from each other. Isra was the first to let go having realized they had been here a while and she was anxious to get things in motion to deal with the matter in hand, with the new knowledge in her possession about Everilda. She had great plans. She wasn't going to tell Contessia yet, but things needed to be thought out and calculated very thoroughly if they were to be successful.

Astrid tensed all of a sudden. She sensed his change in behavior immediately and she had the notion that it had something to do with Contessia. She looked into his dark brown eyes; he quickly realized she was staring right into his soul and he tensed up a little more. He couldn't help it, he was nervous; not of her, but what she was now finding out about him. Astrid had always been good to Isra and he had always been faithful to her as well as a loyal companion so he had nothing to fear from her.

Isra was tuning in to all of his deepest, darkest and most hidden thoughts. That was what made him nervous because nobody else had ever been able to read him before until he had met her.

She stopped for a moment and closed her eyes as she pressed her hand to his forehead and he knew then that she would now know everything. He felt the warmth of her hand on his forehead and the energy that followed as she and he connected in a most divine way. She laughed a little as she opened her eyes and greeted him with a smile, a smile that told him she wasn't mad with him although he had feared that she might have been.

"I should have known. You do like your toys, don't you? Tell me, did our Contessia give you a thrill?" she inquired humorously.

She was quite amused about the situation; neither did she feel he had betrayed her. This made him relax and loosen up as he honestly had no inclination of how she would react upon learning the truth regarding the sinister torture he had inflicted upon Contessia.

"Well, I was playing with her, too. So truly, I do understand but I don't understand why you didn't reveal to me what you were doing," she finished, a little perplexed that he had hid this from her all this time.

He felt quite guilty and tried his utmost to flash a sweet, puppy dog smile but then he realized that he should just be a man about this and admit his act of wrongdoing.

"Well, I knew you had your own agenda with her but I wanted to have a little fun to test her loyalty and it seems the more I did to her, the further away she went from you. Then you took her under your wing and of course she was trapped between the thresholds of both of us," he explained. "It was at that time I stopped because the matter of Everilda and her presence was more important than some silly Wiccan girl who I had been playing mind games with."

Isra looked at him seriously while showing a subtle yet sweet smile. "That silly Wiccan girl has been caught in Everilda's dangerous web," she affirmed gently.

Astrid raised a stern eyebrow as he suddenly felt sympathy for Contessia and was starting to feel bad about what he had done to her. He wasn't one to live in the past so he quickly stopped himself in his train of reminiscent thought.

"So what is to be done?" he questioned as he looked his witch dead in the eyes.

Isra stepped back a little and folded her arms in an independent stance. "I will take care of it." She graciously took his hand and kissed it with her warm, soft lips.

"Don't worry about Contessia. I will do whatever is needed to keep her out of this ghastly plot that Everilda has concocted," Astrid announced firmly.

Isra turned to face him. "I need to go and take care of a couple of things. Please go back home and watch Contessia until I return."

She headed into the trees with Astrid watching her before he continued back to the tower to follow her requested instruction.

18

Isra had gone and off on her way to achieve her mysterious deed and Astrid had almost arrived home. The raven-man's head was full of unrelenting thoughts of what would happen next in this compelling predicament between Isra, Everilda, and now Contessia. He was worried about his witch but all he could do was trust that she knew what she was doing.

Isra had asked him to watch Contessia while she was gone. He was happy to do so without question even though he didn't really like the girl and truly, he felt like Contessia made him and Isra easy targets for the vengeful mortal Everilda. Alas, Astrid was to keep these observations to himself for he didn't want to offend or upset his love.

As Astrid slowly got close to the tall tower and unlocked the ornate wooden door, he began to hear shrieking sounds coming from above and immediately ran up the stairs to investigate.

He saw Contessia immediately. She was in the center of the main lounge, and then he looked more closely and he saw deep, red blood dripping down from the tear ducts on both of her eyes. He was stunned and didn't know what to say. He would have asked her if she was okay, but he quickly realized that would be a rather redundant approach judging from the blood that was slowly forming a small pool on the middle of the natural wood floor.

He also suspected this was the work of Everilda. Well, he was sure it was her. Who else could do something like this? Contessia had hardly any friends to speak of, minus her old clan who had disbanded from her since her association with Lady Isra.

Blood dripping from the eyes? Surely that can't be a coincidence, he thought to himself as he carefully surveyed the situation.

He suddenly paused and looked around to see if anyone was standing behind him, but found it was just him and Contessia. Astrid wasn't sure what was afoot; sure, he could tune in to all the dark and not so dark things of this world, both metaphysical and physical. He knew almost everything to do with the light and the dark and his greatest strength was his gut feeling but sometimes even he was out of his depth when it came to strange phenomena.

Astrid looked at Contessia, who was now on the floor in the puddle of her own blood. Although she was in distress, she seemed cathartic at the sight of it, as if it was cleansing some foul thing from inside her body. She seemed a little breathless and incoherent as she spoke. "I never thought I would be so glad to be in your company." She gasped as she struggled to catch her breath.

She had addressed Astrid personally, which she had never done, as she normally avoided all conversation with the raven-man. He naturally found it strange for her to do so and inferred she must be scared.

"You know, in the greater scheme of things, you're just a pawn for Everilda and I knew sooner or later you would lead her to us, so I am not immensely fond of you either."

He watched the forlorn girl writhing around in the puddle of blood she had created. Although she was in distress, she seemed to enjoy it. The salty blood dripped down from her face to her feet. She was saturated in it. Her eyes were no longer bleeding but there she was, covered in her own ruby red bodily fluid and Astrid watched as she moved her hands all over her body, covering herself in the liquid.

What a strange way to behave, he thought.

Isra had walked for many miles since leaving Astrid to go off on her mission, although she had not disclosed exactly what the mission was. She had refused to divulge this information and had simply said goodbye to Astrid with a kiss.

It was just after midday and she felt the fresh sunshine on her face. She smiled wistfully as she approached a cute and quaint little cottage with honeysuckle delicately wrapped around the door frame. She could see that beyond the door, a young girl with hazelnut hair was sweeping by the front step.

Nothing changes around these parts, she thought wickedly to herself as she watched the girl closely and started to walk toward her.

Lady Isra wasn't a stranger to the inhabitants of this cottage. So, it was of no surprise to Lady Isra when the girl dropped her broom in horror and stared at the witch in shock.

"What do you want with us?" the frightened girl asked, panicking as she felt terror in her veins.

Lady Isra licked her lips wildly as she knew the girl was frightened of her.

The girl watched the witch as she did this and started to feel an immense air of panic, wondering what the witch wanted and when she would go away, *if* she would go away. Isra laughed as she read the girl's thoughts.

"I'm here because you owe me," she announced sharply.

You see, Isra had come here because the girl, whose name was Cora, greatly owed Isra because of something that had happened long ago and now Isra was here to collect on that debt. She hadn't walked all of these miles just to admire the cottage and its scenery!

No, she had come here to collect on that debt from their past and to make Cora useful, although she used that term mildly as she didn't have much use for a girl like Cora. It was funny as even though Cora was probably around twenty-six years of age now, she had not changed at all. Still the same brown hair that lingered below her shoulders in a cropped low fashion, not that Cora had any style to speak of.

Cora began to panic again but this time Isra noticed and reassured her. "Oh, don't worry yourself so. I'm not here to kill you, child! Let's face it; you'd be of no use to me that way! No, I'm here because you know of ways to own somebody's soul."

Cora's heart skipped a beat in her chest. *Soul magic?* she thought to herself. *That hasn't been used in years and there is no way my father would allow it. But why would Lady Isra of all dark and ghastly witches want to own somebody's soul?*

Cora stopped her thoughts as she remembered Isra could hear them, and she didn't want to accidentally place herself in the heart of the witch's wrath.

"Soul magic is forbidden in these parts," she asserted firmly, noticing Lady Isra's piercing green gaze was all over her.

Lady Isra laughed and she hissed at Cora. "Yes, it may be forbidden but I know you can do it. I also know of many things that are supposedly forbidden yet people seem to manage to do them quite effectively, even with that being so," Isra pointed out forcefully.

Cora quickly relented, knowing there was no arguing with Isra. "Okay, whose soul do you want ownership of?" She picked her broom up and placed it against the cottage wall, realizing Lady Isra wasn't going to leave until she had what she came for.

"May I come in?" Isra inquired.

Cora quickly replied, "All right, come on in. I'll make some tea."

Isra smiled as she ventured into the quaint little cottage and sat herself down in a comfortable chair. She noticed the room was dim with only natural light that barely got through the dull, old windows as Cora brought in a pot of tea and two cups on a silver tray. She found it funny that Cora, being as poor as she was, had a silver tea tray in her possession and focused her verbal attention on when Cora placed it on the table.

"My child, have times changed for you? I don't believe I recall you being able to afford silver."

"It's a family heirloom from my father's side," Cora said defensively, trying her best to tolerate the witch's remark.

Cora was very defensive when it came to her family, especially her father. She hated when people mocked him. Cora's father was a wise, proud man who had done a lot of bad things in his time that, in her eyes, were justified. She believed he still had done right and had good intentions despite what had happened.

He had been exiled by the village council and could no longer live with Cora, as he feared for her safety. He felt that if he was present in their home village or if somebody possessed the knowledge that he was in the village, Cora could be kidnapped, tortured, and maybe even killed by the villagers as a way of getting to him.

The outrage that came from the villagers combined with a forceful vengeance toward him ultimately made him leave his daughter behind. Cora hated that. She hated that her father had to leave her to face their world alone but she couldn't change what had happened. She had no choice but to live with it, much to her annoyance and hatred, as she really missed her father.

She had originally wanted to go with him but he sternly told her that he didn't want that life for her. A life where they would always be looking over their shoulder and fearing the day they would be found and then killed. Cora knew what her father had done. She knew he had unleashed some of the most dangerous and frowned upon acts of magics unto this world. The very same dangerous magics that Lady Isra had sought Cora out for today.

Cora paused as she knew the witch was quite possibly reading her thoughts and she wanted their meeting over and done with as soon as time could allow it to be so. She poured the tea simultaneously into both cups before sitting herself down at the seat opposite Lady Isra and then she asked the question that she knew she had to ask if she wanted Lady Isra to go away pronto.

"Whose soul are you looking to gain ownership of?" she inquired again as Lady Isra carefully watched Cora's facial movements.

Isra did not trust Cora and more importantly, she didn't want the sweet little cottage girl warning anyone that she shouldn't before she gained ownership of her desired soul.

"My dear child," she started formally as she formed her lips close together with both her eyes still on Cora. "You do not need to know the details, just draw up the soul possession contract with the spell and I will be on my merry way!" She looked Cora dead on eye level.

Cora was hesitant at the prospect of not knowing whose soul she was going to be giving to Lady Isra but she thought better of it, knowing that once it was done, Isra would be on her way. She felt inconsolably guilty about this but decided it would be in her best interest to just do it. Yes, she was doing a terrible thing, giving somebody like Isra the power to control another by owning their soul, but if it got her out of Lady Isra's fiery web, she'd do anything to stay out of harm's way.

Isra was getting inpatient. She could see Cora didn't want to do the ghastly deed but she wasn't vacating the land until Cora had fulfilled her end of the bargain. She tapped her fingers hastily on the table as she watched the hesitation on Cora's face. She could see Cora was doing her utmost to avoid doing the needed ritual right away but she could see through the girl very clearly.

Cora tried to be casual when she explained to Isra that she needed to go to her sacred room to invoke the spirits and complete this task but Isra was not convinced by her body language and decided to follow her uninvited to her precious, sacred place. Cora tried to be as casual as possible despite the invasive intrusion from Lady Isra. She led Isra up the long winding wooden staircase, nodding at Isra when they both reached the top and she stood back to reveal a black velvet curtain concealing her beloved room.

Isra immediately came to the conclusion that this must be the exact place Cora's father had inhabited while invoking some of the darkest and deadliest magics known to the universe. She quietly imagined Cora's father kneeling on the floor invoking the spirits and working late into the night to accomplish many terrible and vile things he would have completed during his tenure in dark soul magic.

Cora slowly lifted the curtain that revealed the much protected and deeply hidden room, showing the deep, black velvet walls that shadowed a small circular table that could barely be seen surrounded by all the black.

Isra inhaled a deep breath as she took in the splendid sights of this wonderful yet mystical and hidden room. She was flabbergasted. She was amazed that someone such as Cora possessed such an outlet to power but didn't do anything to claim it.

She thought of Cora as slightly mad, because for someone with a widely known occult background, she could have been anything but instead she chose to be just a timid cottage girl living in her father's shadow. Isra felt quite unwelcome as she felt her way across the deep, black walls, feeling the energies that once existed here.

Cora looked on as Isra tapped into these energies and shuddered as she felt a notion she had not felt for many years.

19

Astrid's patience was wavering. He had been here for several hours now standing guard of Contessia and letting her get on with her act of possession as she immersed herself in her own blood.

He thought it was rather pointless and that the girl was just doing it for his attention. He didn't like Contessia. He felt she was unstable, an atomic bomb that could explode at any moment. She was lethal, in his perception.

He strongly feared that Lady Isra hadn't considered how dangerous it was to have Contessia under her roof; she was connected to not only Klinq, the gnome who had worked for Isra for a little while, but also Isra's old nemesis, Everilda.

Lady Isra had only recently discovered that Everilda was using Contessia to try to gain her power, to take Isra down, but none of this bothered Isra. She knew Everilda would go to the most desperate lengths she could in order to try and take her down. She empathized with the word "try."

Isra wasn't easily beaten. She knew Everilda and she knew how she worked. Everilda resorted to mind games and getting down and dirty with tricks and deceptions, whereas Isra was straight up and honest. Yes, she may have been venomous and intimidating in her approach, but she never let you think that you were a friend when she knew she was far from that and never would be.

Astrid thought back to Everilda's grand entrance where she had appeared in a flash of lightning and thunderclaps. He had to admit, he had been fooled as before he saw the light show Everilda had put on, he had believed it was Isra. Alas, even Astrid with all his insight could still be fooled. He wasn't proud of this moment when he had slipped and almost mistaken Everilda for Isra, but he wasn't always one to admit when he was wrong.

Astrid kept his faults very much to himself. He believed he would be persecuted if he revealed them out in the open. He wasn't sure that someone as powerful as Isra would like him as much as she did if she knew all he had done in his past. He was very down on himself over it and a little insecure at times.

He was thrilled when she revealed she was fond of him. He was absolutely ecstatic that Isra with all her power, who could have chosen anyone, wanted *him*. He thought she may have said no. He thought she may have not been ready for the commitment that true love required. He thought he was the luckiest man alive when she uttered those words, "I need you here."

That day had been the happiest in his life. He'd had some real magical ones, but that day topped them all! He had never felt so privileged to be in her realm, in her world, and for him to be the guest in hers! He felt a sense of sentiment fill his veins as he realized he was still standing over Contessia and that he had been day dreaming.

He had grown tired of Contessia over the last few weeks; he wanted her out of the way, out of Isra's and his lives! He wanted her gone. Transported to a foreign place, where she would never be able to return! He had often thought about expressing this notion to Isra but thought better of it when he realized she had her own plans for the girl.

Astrid stood back watching Contessia as she was deep in her own form of trance. She had her fingernails scraping deep into the floorboards, drawing at what laid beneath them in a warrior stance with her shoulders bent as she crouched over.

He pulled at the girl and yanked her out of her blood puddle while facing her. She was startled, quickly realizing she was covered in thick, red liquid. She had no memory of how she had come to be this way or even why she was covered in her own blood!

It caused her to be overwhelmed and she screeched, "Why is there blood all over me? Is it mine?"

Astrid held her firmly against the wall as he spoke in a deep and harsh voice. "I came back from waving Isra on her travels to find you here in that puddle and you were quite happily playing and writhing around on the floor, covered in *that*!"

He pointed at the blood puddle as she looked on in horror. She didn't remember any of it. She was grossed out as she knew the raven-man wasn't lying. She had been playing in the blood. She also had been thoroughly immersing herself in it and enjoying herself while exposed to its rich, salty taste and texture.

She felt uncontrollably sick. Her stomach danced with cataclysmic spasms. How could something like this mess with her in such a way? To control her and make her do these things that she would never do in a normal circumstance? She thought she was going mad. Maybe she was. She wanted to know what the game was and why she was doing these things, then having no memory of the event occurring.

She didn't understand any of it. She didn't understand why the strangest and most awful things kept happening to her. She looked at Astrid for some kind of validation that she wasn't going crazy. The raven-man solemnly didn't give it. He had no intention of reassuring her or being her friend.

He coldly looked back at her and uttered, "We need to find a way to keep you out of harm's way while this demon works its way through your delicate mind!"

He wasn't being tactful, he knew that. Tact wasn't in the forefront of his mind. He knew Contessia was a problem and that Everilda would strike at nothing to attain what she thought was hers. It was only a matter of time before she struck again.

He had really meant he would need to find a way to keep Contessia from bringing forth more trouble for Isra, but he didn't use that wording for his meaning. However, unbeknown to him, Isra was already away doing just that.

Isra and Cora were both in a serene, mist of concentration as they both knelt at opposite sides of the circular table focusing their gaze on each other as a vibrant pink and green vortex was suspended above their heads. It was as electrifying as the energy danced in the air. Pink sparks were projecting everywhere in bold contrast to the black room. They were so focused on their dynamic task that their eyes didn't flicker or blink, not once. Both magic practitioners transfixed, emitting powerful energy to accomplish the goal at hand.

Cora's hands lay on the table at each side, mirroring Lady Isra's on her side of it. Their eyes met in the center, focused and engaged. You would have never guessed that these two women weren't particularly fond of each other, the way their eyes met in a reminiscent gaze!

As Lady Isra and Cora kept their concentration, the vortex above them increased in size so now it was almost covering the entire ceiling. Both women seemed intrigued as the pink and green energy continued to flourish, firing off bolts of gold lightning all over. Cora's sacred room was suddenly looking like a carnival of spectacular fireworks, which was unusual, since it was always black.

Their eyes watched intrusively as the magic emitted its rays from the top of the ceiling. Cora met Lady Isra's gaze in a circle of wondrous mystery as she suddenly understood the reason why Lady Isra had asked for her assistance. She was going to take an innocent witch's soul without their permission and without their asking! She wanted to know more but she was getting weary and her eyes were losing their focus. They were beginning to close. All she could see was this girl being trapped by the formidable witch and she wanted to cry out, she wanted to scream but she couldn't.

It was too late and there was nothing she could do; even if she broke the magic now, it was going to be inevitable. The girl's fate would be sealed!

It was with this sudden insight that Cora at once dropped back down into the depths of reality and the magic ended. Her eyes opened at once. She felt the pain in her head screeching. It was unbearable. It pounded against her skull. Hammering. Screaming.

She held her head in her hands as the pain grew, focusing directly on the center of her brain. It began to swell in size, forming into a circle that went all the way round as it intensified dramatically. This pain gave Cora a very quick reminder that this is what happens when you assist another in the business of evil.

This was the price she paid for helping Lady Isra wrongfully gain control of another's soul. A soul that had no knowledge of what was taking place and didn't know what her fate was going to be! If she did, she'd run like hell!

Lady Isra had now come to and was aware of everything. She knew Cora had broken the magic but it didn't matter as it was done. She stood proudly, surveying the scene before her. Cora stood facing the wall, holding her head in a violent outburst of pain. Cora wasn't in Isra's interest, however. She was more interested in what the magic had created.

The vortex that was above them previously was now just a golden shimmer glowing in the center of the room, dominating everything in it. As Lady Isra moved closer to the golden centerpiece, she caught sight of a long, carefully wrapped scroll, hovering in midair above it. It called to her with its calligraphy-style handwriting dancing across the paper, highlighting the red blood splatters that appeared at opposite ends of the scroll.

Lady Isra grabbed the scroll excitedly, unwrapping it, revealing its glorious contents. She was beaming with a healthy glow as she smiled. It was a smile that said, "I have won." She felt triumphant as her eyes fell upon the handwriting that was hastily smeared across the paper.

Lady Isra looked back at Cora and regained her composure ahead of her excitement as she uttered, "Our business is done, Cora. I don't need you anymore! But if you tell anyone about our dealings here, you don't need me to tell you what will happen to you if you disregard my warning!"

Then Isra paused as she thought of something else. She licked her lips and smiled as she couldn't believe she had almost forgotten something very important.

She then added, "And not forgetting, your beloved father!" she threatened although there was a hint of sweetness in her threat.

Cora didn't need telling twice. She was nervous at Lady Isra's threat but she knew she could never tell. She didn't care about her life but she did care about the life of her father! She would do anything to see him still breathing.

"I will not breathe a word to anyone," she said firmly.

Isra looked at her and tapped her fondly on the chin. "Of course, you won't, child!" she chided sarcastically as she smiled and then turned to leave.

Still holding the scroll in her hand, she waved goodbye and then vanished.

Cora watched as Isra made her way down the steps and closed the cottage door behind her as she went out. Cora felt free. The pain in her head had disappeared too. She breathed a heavy sigh of relief. *Phew, she's finally gone,* she thought to herself.

Now she would never have to deal with the wretched Lady Isra of the Dark ever again!

Lady Isra made haste on her journey home. She had much to prepare. The scroll was in her hand and so was the soul she now owned! Of course, the existing owner of that soul was completely clueless to the array of events that had just conspired but now Isra knew. She knew she was guaranteed to win.

She smiled. She observed the night sky making its appearance. The moon was making her presence known, slowly rising up like a snow topped sun. She thought of Astrid. She couldn't wait to get home to him so she could tell him the news.

Astrid sat comfortably on the couch. He had a book half open, turned on its spine. It was placed across his knee, his legs relaxed and resting on the cushion of the couch. He had been reading but his thoughts, as always, had interrupted his evening.

His thoughts were loud and expressive. He had been thinking about Isra. He thought about how much he missed her. He wondered if she had managed to find a solution for their Contessia problem.

Contessia mystified and annoyed Astrid at the best of times, but today he had lost his patience with her. He had witnessed her bewitched. She was not herself. She was under a truly malevolent spell. He had quickly seen the state she was in and pulled her out of her weary consciousness. One yank with his firm grip was all that was needed. He had been cold and harsh toward her. She was hurt by his coarse words but more so by the truth they contained.

Contessia was a fragile soul. She believed in love and beauty and all things good. She wasn't used to criticism or someone berating her. Astrid had berated her in a sense but he saw her as a problem, one that needed to be dealt with immediately. It was no secret he didn't like her. He was waiting for the moment when they could get rid of her. He felt she was trouble.

He was sitting on the couch thinking about this difficult matter when a very visual image literally jumped into his head! Yes, it jumped! He thought this was strange although he should've been used to bizarre phenomena by now.

It was Lady Isra. His Isra. She clearly stood in the center of a bleak, misty cemetery. Astrid noticed that the spot surrounding Isra was enchanted. All the leaves were falling from the trees but only in that one circular space, the space that Lady Isra was standing in. The rest of the cemetery stayed still. Almost silent. It was serene yet captivating.

His thoughts were solely focused on this image of Isra in this ghostly vision, standing alone in this place. He couldn't figure out why he was seeing it. Was she sending it to him telepathically? He closed his eyes, connecting with the visual image in his mind. It became clearer. Stronger. Almost as though she was in Technicolor!

The vision quickly faded. He paid it no mind. His focus had shifted. His mind was distracted and somewhat perplexed. His head was elsewhere. All he could think of was that Isra would be home soon.

Something interrupted his thoughts. He suddenly felt like he wasn't alone in the room. He moved his head around nervously, looking for what it might be. He could hear something nearby and jolted out of his seated position on the couch.

A black cat appeared and promptly sat beside him on the couch. It was Onyx, the kitten he had given to Isra as a gift. He had grown considerably. Astrid smiled as the cat made himself at home next to Astrid's legs.

He muttered to the animal, "You're missing your mommy, aren't you?" as he scratched the cat's head. "And missing the life you were so used to before you came to us, no doubt."

Onyx was busily preening himself as Astrid had an intriguing thought. *What about Klinq? How does Klinq fit into this scenario?*

He hadn't given the gnome much thought for some time but now it had occurred to him that maybe Klinq had appeared in his thoughts for a reason. His thoughts often gave him insight into the most otherworldly and complex problems. It was his unique way of thinking that gave him an ability to figure things out. It gave him an edge. It was an asset to him, a part of his personality that made him Astrid.

Astrid thought back to when Lady Isra had seen Klinq and Everilda in a fiery confrontation. She had also learned that Everilda and Klinq were in cahoots with each other, adding Contessia as Everilda's deadly pawn into the mix.

Isra had left the scene with a new-found well of knowledge at her disposal, feeling triumphant that there was nothing Everilda could use against her, because now she knew everything. And there was nothing about Everilda and her plot that Isra didn't know. Now Klinq had vanished out of the limelight, disappearing without a trace!

Astrid thought, *This is very odd, why would he just disappear? Surely, he would remain in the forefront while being badgered by Everilda, being commanded to her every need and whim.*

Klinq was a coward. He would run away from anything. He was

born frightened. He had disappointed Contessia, his only friend. He had shamed his family. He had upset Lady Isra. He had also made the fatal mistake of defying the notorious Everilda! That was probably his worst decision he could have made.

Astrid was now wondering where Klinq could be. He thought that if he could find Klinq's whereabouts, maybe he could force some home truths out of the gnome. That could also help Isra in her forthcoming battle. The question was, where was Klinq likely to be? Astrid was going to find out.

Astrid turned to Onyx. "I am going to have to leave you, my boy," he expressed sympathetically before scratching Onyx's head. Onyx paid no attention and curled himself into a black ball in response.

He smirked at the cat's reaction and then thought, *So much for my relaxing evening!*

He remembered the book he had placed across his knee. Now was not a time for leisurely reading. He reached for the book. His fingers caressed the pages as it closed. He stood up, lifting his legs from their comfortable station on the couch, flexing his muscles as he reached up. The book loosened from his grip as he situated it back on the shelf.

He stared at himself in the mirror, feeling a little perplexed. He lifted his shirt up, revealing his toned stomach. He patted it, giving himself a cheeky half smile. He then focused on his facial features in the mirror. Touching his eyes, he felt no bags underneath them. As a raven, he never had a human face. It still sparked his curiosity. He touched his skin and felt the roughness of his facial hair. He was distracted. He knew this. His mind ran away with him.

He put his fingers to his lips and paused. He would have to think strategically if he was going to find Klinq! That was certain.

20

Astrid knew he had to put his thinking cap on immediately. He knew he'd have to get his brain in gear. Something to get the cogs whirring. The wheels are turning. Something that touched his focus, mentally speaking.

He quickly decided on what he needed: his favorite beverage since he had been human. His beloved friend, coffee! Astrid loved coffee. Some would say he loved coffee more than he loved people.

Coffee could get Astrid through the most complicated of situations. He had become quite accustomed to it since he had been transformed into human form. It was a daily habit that had developed not long after Lady Isra transformed him into a man. It happened purely by chance. Just like their meeting!

One day, he had smelt this wondrous aroma that was so fragrant it reminded him of the earth, and he asked, "What is that?"

She replied while laughing, "Why, that is coffee. Would you like to try some?"

And he did and he had been hooked ever since. It amazed him how one beverage could be so frightfully good and yet so delectably addictive. He was passionate about coffee as much as he was passionate about Isra.

He tapped his finger meticulously as the kettle boiled fiercely on the stove. The steam filled his nostrils. His senses heightened without a filter, patiently waiting for the magical stove to concoct the tantalizing taste conundrum.

He paused for a moment to add the coffee beans to his cup. The smell of the beans was overpowering and bitter at the same time. He liked the bitterness. He wasn't really a fan of anything too sweet or sugary. He liked things that were bitter. He liked them purely for the authenticity they possessed. He adored the harsh reality of things.

He wasn't really one who shimmied along, dancing to the delights of fairy tales. He preferred reality over fantasy but he did practice magic and he understood magic, even before he'd met Isra. Astrid was born and raised in a nest where magic really was a remarkable and miraculous thing! Raised in a crowded nest with his brother, his sister and his mother who was very much a spiritual being, Astrid had been taught incredibly early on that magic was a part of life. It was a part of nature. They knew this to be fundamentally true!

Astrid's mother had done her utmost to impress her knowledge of magic and the world's mysticism upon her three children, but only Astrid and his brother had truly gotten it. They understood it. They went out and experienced magic for themselves. They knew it to be powerful and dangerous at the same time. They knew what it could do, and they knew what not to do with it. They studied the spiritual ways and they became familiar with the customs and respected the ancestors.

They would often receive counsel from the elder ravens and were educated on magic and mysticism by these magnificent creatures. Although the lessons seemed boring for the two young male ravens at times, they did prove to be astonishingly meaningful.

Astrid's sister had died shortly after hatching but his sister's death gave him a strong and potent philosophy on life which was: Live strong. Be good. Be positive. And live the best life you can!

He never forgot his sister. He had his memories. But it was because of her death he knew that life could end at any time and it was important to make the best of it. It taught him a lot about life. It made him stronger. It also hardened him inside but he never saw any harm in it. He knew as a raven life was tough. Nature was cruel. So, he found it easier on his soul to be tough.

Astrid took a big gulp of his coffee. It was warm and soothing despite the bittersweet taste. He quickly realized it was too hot and it burnt the tip of his tongue but then it came to him! A very potent vision. Images appearing slowly. Astrid's eyes were open but he could see it unfolding in his head! It was Klinq. He wouldn't even have to look for him now because he could see exactly where he was! He knew his exact location.

There he was, wandering around the forest, close to where Contessia's clan was situated. In this visionary image, Klinq was tired and forlorn. He had been moving from place to place. Many days traveling had brought his energy levels to a minimum. He was carrying a cloth sack upon his shoulder, held in place with his weary hand.

Astrid watched with his eyes open as Klinq took a moment to rest. Klinq dropped his sack to the floor as he sat on the grass, the sun gently peering through his hat that covered his head. Astrid took a novel approach to this and snapped his fingers. He paused as he waited for the change, closing his eyes and visualizing his arms as long feathered black wings. Within seconds, Astrid was in his raven form again!

He took flight out of the open window. His feathers delicately brushed against the clouds as he circled the moody skies, moving quickly as he scanned the world below him. Looking for his target. His eyes activated his inner superpower. He scanned the area for signs of the runaway gnome. His eyes were peeled for any sightings of him.

He would find the gnome and then he would bring him to Isra. That would please her. He always wanted to keep Isra happy. He would do anything to keep her happy.

It didn't take Astrid long to find Klinq. There he saw the gnome on his laurels and sat upon the grass. He laughed as he disembarked from his winged flight. He landed beside Klinq and the gnome looked at Astrid at a loss. He seemed to be in a bit of a mix up. He didn't understand what the raven was doing here and why it was looking at him.

He petted Astrid's head and said, "Can I help you, my fine fellow?"

Subsequently after Klinq had said those fateful words, Astrid physically answered his question. The grass blades shifted. The earth shook. Klinq looked to the earth for signs of validation. Perhaps he was praying for his salvation!

A black energy surrounded Astrid, covering his entire bird body, and then the raven morphed into a man. The man now stared at Klinq. Klinq stared back, shocked at how such a thing could transpire!

"Actually, you can!" Astrid announced.

"Oh, I should have known it was you!" Klinq stuttered, shocked that he was talking to Astrid all this time. He thought it was just another raven. And ravens were pretty common around these parts, or so he thought!

Astrid looked so cross. He could explode at any moment! "Save your blubbering for the witch! We knew you were up to no good, and here you are! Hiding in the shadow of night."

He gave Klinq eye contact as they both stood facing each other in the dead of night.

"It is no surprise that I've caught you here. And you were working for Everilda all the time, long before you found your way to the tower of Lady Isra!"

Oh, now the raven turned man was becoming real cranky. His cheeks reddened as he continued his fiery interrogation of Klinq. Klinq was in trouble. Astrid wasn't going to let him get off easily! It was unknown at this point whether Klinq would make it through this alive.

Astrid would pummel the gnome. Tear him down. Wrestle him to the ground if he had to if that was the only choice available. To compel the gnome to confess the truth, that is what Astrid would do! Astrid took no prisoners. He didn't suffer fools gladly. He didn't take kindly to deceit either. Klinq would have to spill his guts out or face the unsightly consequences!

Klinq stammered as he paced three steps back away from Astrid.

Astrid humored his behavior and jeered at Klinq sarcastically. Klinq was now starting to really piss Astrid off. Not only had he lied, but he and Isra had given the gnome a place in their home; sure it was just a dingy old basement, but it was a home nonetheless! They had also given Klinq their trust which he had repaid by meeting with Everilda in secret and passing on every single piece of action that was happening in their midst.

Astrid stared at the gnome solemnly as he spoke. "Do you really think that's going to help you? I'm bringing you to Lady Isra and there, my dear fellow, you will confess all or face her wrath! Believe me; you will not want to face her wrath. You know how she feels about betrayal!"

Astrid marched right up to Klinq. He got closer with every step. He proceeded to grab the gnome, yanking his arm severely, almost pulling it out of its socket as he did so. Klinq felt the pain as Astrid held him in his impenetrable grip. The raven-man had a tight hold on the gnome's arm and there was no feasible way for him to escape it!

Klinq made a complaint, but Astrid let his moans fall on deaf ears and told him, "Shut up! You engineered this. Now you face the consequences of your actions! She is not going to be too thrilled when she sees you!"

Klinq held his head down. He was silent for the rest of the journey back to the tower of Lady Isra. He thought about the raven-man's words.

I'm doomed. She's going to kill me. She's going to make mincemeat out of me! Fuck! I'm dead! he thought gravely.

Whichever way he looked at it, he was inevitably doomed. He had sealed his own fate! He was going to have to face up to what he had done whether he liked it or not! The realization of this was setting in far too painfully.

Isra, meanwhile, was almost home. She had traveled silently through the night. It took her almost four hours to walk from Cora's village to her land in the forest. She felt satisfied despite the long journey. Her feet ached from the trudge but she kept walking nonetheless.

Isra had no clue that Astrid had taken matters into his own claws and had sought out Klinq. She was oblivious to the raven-man's plan but she couldn't wait to tell her companion the wonderful news that they would win the battle! Or more pointedly, that she would win!

When the time came for Isra and Everilda to come ablaze in a fiery fire ball, Isra wanted to take down Everilda herself. She wanted to see Everilda fall with no interference from anybody! Yes, she was allowing Astrid to assist her but when it came to the cataclysm; she wanted it just to be her and Everilda! It was very much a personal matter! Isra was looking forward to sharing this triumph with Astrid, of course.

The night skies looked serene as Isra walked through the trees. She walked gracefully as her midnight blue cloak softly dragged behind her, the velvet fabric clinging to the woodland floor with every step she took. She looked up at the sky with complete fascination as she admired it fondly. The stars blinked at her as they illuminated their radiance across the sky. They were so bright on this night despite the blackened void. They looked almost ablaze, like an aurora borealis but with no incandescent colors!

Astrid and Klinq were just approaching the grounds of Lady Isra's tower. They had chosen to hasten their voyage for a few moments as Klinq had been grumbling about his foot hurting which Astrid didn't believe but still allowed Klinq to rest for a moment. Neither Astrid nor Klinq was aware of it, but Isra was only moments away from them!

Isra hummed to herself all the while blissfully strolling amongst tall blades of overgrown grass. Her fingers gently brushed against the tips as she passed through. The blades delicately touched her skin.

She felt calm and relaxed. She was feeling peace and serenity. Her mind was blank and complacent.

Voices nearby caught her interest. She gazed ahead, catching sight of two figures. One of the figures stopped as he gazed at her. Her eyes met his as she realized it was Astrid.

21

She began walking with fond anticipation toward her lover. His eyes were all over her as she approached. He was spellbound as he inspected her from afar, watching her from every angle. He had to admit from whichever side she was on, the view was indeed a pleasant one!

He noted her slender frame that stood out in her cloak in the deepest shade of blue. Her delicate but tiny waist. Her long fair hair with elegant curls that framed her face. Not a single hair was out of place.

As she got closer, he noticed a sweet smile appear on her face. Happy to see him. She was delighted to be in his presence. It filled him with hunger. He couldn't wait for his lips to greet hers. For her to know he had missed her. He just simply couldn't wait to kiss her!

She now stood inches before him, her fingers ready to touch him. She anticipated his touch. Her eyes let him know that she was his!

Klinq looked on as the couple admired each other instinctively. He wished he could be someplace else but being held by Astrid, he had no choice but to stay put as they embraced each other with sensual imagery.

Their eyes met in a thoughtful gaze. Astrid and Isra's hands slowly linked as one. Astrid, still with his firm grip on Klinq, straightened his stance as he allowed his free arm to glide around Isra's waist and he planted his moist kiss on her lips.

Isra pulled Astrid away gently, holding his hand in her own. She wanted to move forward. There were more important matters at hand. She held his hand and bestowed upon it a kiss. One that let him know he had been truly missed. His love in her eyes was perfect unadulterated bliss.

She turned her immediate attention to Klinq as she stepped away from Astrid. "So, it seems we have ourselves a troublesome gnome!"

She laughed as Klinq looked as if he might choke on her words. He was horrified to see her standing before him in her full splendor. He had no idea of what she was intending to do with him or more painfully to him!

Astrid interrupted her with a smile, "Yes, I brought him for you."

She smiled wickedly at the raven-man's gesture. She loved it when he did things for her. Out of thought for her! He truly went above and beyond to keep her satisfied and satisfied.

"How sweet of you!" she uttered and then stopped as she remembered Contessia. "I would say we should lock him up in the basement, but that won't be empty for very long!" she hinted. Astrid wasn't quite sure what she meant.

Astrid followed his instinct and asked, "Why can't I just throw this ghastly thing into the basement?"

He looked at Klinq as he said this which only heightened Klinq's fear. Of course, this was a deliberate move on the part of Astrid. He enjoyed making the gnome sweat. Some would say Astrid enjoyed it a little too much.

Isra smiled at Astrid. "Wait and see, for all good things have a time and precedence! I have to go see Contessia now! Be a dear and keep this one under strict watch while I attend to that."

She then proceeded to open her large ornate tower door and disappeared from sight. Astrid and Klinq were left perplexed with only their curiosity to guide them as to what she was up to. But only Isra knew!

Isra found Contessia sitting on the couch as she entered the lounge. She smiled at her as Contessia smiled back at her weakly. She didn't hesitate. She wasn't going to let this drag on any further. It was time. Contessia was going to be in Isra's possession within moments of her signing the scroll!

She reached into her cloak and pulled out the scroll, holding it out as she began to speak. "So, I've found the cause for your ailment, my dear girl. All we need to secure your safety is a protection spell! I have drawn up all the relevant documentation. Now all I need you to do is to sign the scroll."

Contessia didn't know what to say. She felt baffled but also relieved as her nightmare would now be over, or so she thought!

"And this is the only way to help me?" Contessia inquired, feeling great emotion and a lot of fear within herself over what had been occurring.

Isra held the scroll closer and stood close to Contessia. She stood, gazing thoughtfully at her and knowing that this was the moment. This was the clinch! That when she had her captivated enough to believe her, that would be it. Isra would own Contessia's soul and then the gloves would be off. War could finally begin between Isra and Everilda!

Contessia could be kept safe out of the way and Isra could begin her tremendous battle. The rest would take care of itself after she had ownership of Contessia. She desperately needed Contessia to sign that scroll and sign her life away to her, even though she didn't know the full detail of what that would entail right now.

"Yes child, so do be a dear and sign it!" she said thoughtfully, waiting to see if Contessia was convinced enough to indeed sign it.

The tension was heating up as the two females eyed each other up, not truly knowing what the other was thinking. Isra saw this as a battle of sheer determination and wit. She was determined to get Contessia's signature on that scroll!

Contessia was apprehensive as you might expect, but Isra knew she was on to a winner. Contessia had no choice but to sign it. What other better offer did she have? She had no friends to speak of, no family to guide her. Her clan had long let go of her since she had become acquainted with Lady Isra. Isra and Astrid were her only contacts and Isra was deemed as close as a sister could be to Contessia.

She thought to herself, *Well, I really can't do any worse here!*

Contessia looked up at once. She took the scroll from Isra's hand. Isra looked on, smiling as Contessia held the scroll. She felt its energy as she held it. It was hot. She could feel the heat rising from it. She felt the power that had cultivated from it. She felt its bright, golden energy surrounding her.

She unraveled the scroll and let her fingers feel their way down to the bottom line. It was enchanted. She could tell. It was magically guiding her hand to the bottom line, where she would inevitably sign her life away. The energy was potent. It was deliberately making sure that she did exactly that.

A pen appeared, floating in midair. Contessia snatched the pen. It swiftly guided her hand down to the bottom line where she scrawled her signature. It was done and dusted! Lady Isra looked on triumphantly as Contessia handed the scroll back to her. She now had full ownership of Contessia's soul!

Isra took a moment to appreciate having the scroll in her hand. It was burning. The fiery golden shimmer set off huge sparks, almost like sparkly stars being emitted from an unknown source. She glanced at Contessia and smiled, knowing that their transaction was now complete. There wasn't much to do with Contessia now but Isra maintained her composure toward her newly acquired possession.

She held her head up high with great integrity as she spoke. "I'm glad things have been attended to! Will you be all right up here? I have to speak with Astrid on a couple of choice matters." Isra proceeded to leave the room.

Contessia nodded solemnly, not uttering a single word. She was silent. She acted like her power to converse had been taken away. Her voice was still there and nothing came out. She didn't understand what had happened to her. She seemed to be in a cationic state as she sat on the couch motionless, her mind and body in a sedated state as she remained physically conscious.

Contessia was illuminated all of a sudden. She had an inner glow all around her aura. It was golden just like the intense magic that dwelled inside the enchanted scroll. Isra looked at her subject bemused, chuckling to herself. Contessia really had no clue as to what was going on!

She daintily strode down her long winding steps, her cloaking dragging behind her. As she glided to the bottom, she found Astrid waiting for her patiently. He stood valiant and true, a knight that had been waiting a lifetime for his one true love. He had a smug yet sweet smile on his face.

He took her hand in his and gently pressed his lips down on her warm, soft skin. She was waiting to see the reason behind his cheeky smile. She could feel his pulse rising with intoxicating pleasure as she allowed him to release her hand. He held her close to him, feeling her warmth as he kissed her. He used his kiss as the perfect opportunity to probe her with a question.

"Are you going to let me in on this mystery that you are keeping under wraps?" he inquired as he felt he was cross-examining her by using a kiss as a way of attaining hidden knowledge.

Isra stared at him wide eyed, feeling his eyes all over her in the tranquil place where it was simply just him and her alone. Astrid firmly pressed against her body, sensing her energy. Feeling her out. Using his incredible foresight to examine every metaphysical inch of her. To seek out and extract that which she was keeping a secret from him.

He was using every resource he had inside of himself to seek out her most unfathomable thoughts. He knew she was up to something. She had been secretive around him recently. He knew she had creatively engineered a commodity featuring Contessia. He knew that something was brewing but as she had not revealed anything to him and he didn't know what it was. He would simply have to wait for Isra to reveal all!

Isra straightened her stance, eyeing him with a playful look and remarked, "I know that you know some things already, but I like how you work to unravel the answer behind the mystery."

"It's my conviction," he whispered in her ear as she showed a small smile.

"Well, there is one thing I haven't told you. Contessia, more precisely, her soul is now in my possession. I own her," Isra finished as Astrid looked surprised at this development.

Wow, she really is taking things to the next level. I wonder what she will do with Contessia now, Astrid thought to himself.

"And what are you going to do with her?!" Astrid questioned as he knew Contessia was a problem to both him and Isra.

He had never wanted to express the notion for fear of offending his witch. He had watched her and he had seen she found some fondness for the Wiccan girl. Not much, however but some.

Isra flashed Astrid her best wicked smile as she touched his bottom lip with her tongue teasingly before announcing, "We do have a very vacant basement that could do with a new occupant."

Astrid chuckled unmercifully at the thought of this. Another prisoner, how fun! He realized his favorite toy, Contessia, was going to be under his control as Lady Isra would no doubt want him in charge of her keep, just as she had with Kane.

Astrid was stopped in mid thought as Isra added, "Every time I go into the basement, I see those beautiful, heavy chains. I hate seeing them just hanging there being neglected. I really wish they would get used!"

Astrid found much hilarity in this and joked, "Chaining her to the wall would give them some use!"

Isra couldn't help but burst out laughing. It was spontaneous, she wasn't expecting it but Astrid did always have that ability to make her laugh!

"I am sure it will! In the meantime, we still have that ghastly gnome in our presence," Isra said wistfully.

Astrid put his fingers to his lips in a thoughtful gesture. "Hmm, why do I get the feeling Klinq and Contessia go together rather nicely in this delightful mix?" he questioned comically as Isra realized what he was hinting toward.

Her face dropped. Her mouth opened in amazement, wildly expressing her joy at remembering this vital detail! *Klinq and Contessia, how sweet!* she thought.

She couldn't believe that she hadn't thought of it any sooner! She remembered Klinq's affection for Contessia. Isra broke her deep train of thought when she realized Astrid was still staring at her, slightly bewildered. She suspected he had been reading her thoughts.

"Oh my! Did you catch me in a wave of thought?" she asked earnestly.

It was with this notion that Astrid pulled Isra closer to him, smiling from ear to ear. He had the cheekiest grin plastered on his face as he uttered, "Oh, I think I caught you in a little bit more than that!"

He winked at her as he held onto her forcefully. It was a tight grip and she could feel the immense pull on her wrists. He wasn't going anywhere. She liked his tight grip on her, the way he could be strong as well as vulnerable. She truly liked every segment of his being.

"I guess we should give Klinq and Contessia a private moment to say their farewells since they won't be seeing each other for a long time!" she uttered malevolently. She was being cold. She wanted to show Klinq how his actions had cost him his only friend and she wasn't going to be kind about it!

"I guess we should," Astrid muttered, letting go of her to carry out this well laid plan.

He didn't waste any time. He went straight for the basement where Klinq had been waiting to know the decision of his fate. Astrid hurried down the steps, opening the basement door swiftly. He didn't hold back on his way as he muttered, "Lady Isra awaits your presence. She won't treat your betrayal lightly! Come on, let's go!"

Astrid's words were solemn and hard. Klinq felt forced as Astrid practically pulled Klinq up from the bed, dragging him towards the steps. It was cold as they marched up the steps. The atmosphere filled with intense dread. The air sent a chill down his back as he felt the fear deeply in his soul. He knew he was in for it.

Astrid marched Klinq to his impending fate when they appeared in the hall. Klinq noted they were by the main door. He didn't understand what was happening but the atmosphere was grim! Klinq was then surprised when Isra appeared out of nowhere beside them. She had Contessia wrapped around her arm. Contessia and Isra acted as if they were sisters.

It all seemed very strange to Klinq. He worried as he stared into Contessia's eyes and glanced fondly at her purple hair. Something came to him, an inner knowing. He knew Contessia wasn't herself. He knew this was some kind of a set-up devised by Lady Isra and Astrid; he just wasn't sure what.

Contessia didn't seem to be conscious of what was going on but she eyed Klinq up suspiciously, wondering what he was doing here, wondering if he was here for her. Of course, he wasn't here for her she thought passively and why would he after all he had done? Abandoning her. Betraying her. And in her mind, letting her go.

She still remembered the day when she and Klinq met. She had coerced him out of his hiding place and had introduced herself to him. She had been welcoming and he seemed calm in her presence. She remembered his gratitude despite his fears as he thanked her and then promptly said goodbye.

Days later, Contessia journeyed to Lady Isra's tower to find him, which she did much to her unpleasantness. It had been a journey she wished she had never taken. Her experience in the tower had been ghastly at best. She could still feel spiders clinging to her body, even though there were none present. She still cringed over that experience.

She wished things could be what they were before. But now she and Klinq were distant. She looked at him and wondered what was left. Maybe he had gone away or maybe Lady Isra was right, that Klinq was indeed a coward.

She noted his nervous demeanor as she stared at him. He shuffled as he was pushed and dragged around, still guarded by Astrid. His every move was watched. Astrid followed Klinq precariously everywhere he went.

22

Contessia watched as Klinq was taken down to the basement. She and Isra followed, although Contessia didn't know why she, Isra, Astrid, and Klinq were all heading for the basement. It was perplexing. She felt a deep sense of foreboding as she entered the dimly lit room.

Klinq was made to stand just inside the basement as Contessia was brought in by Isra. Isra immediately vacated the room, her presence not being needed, for now. Astrid took full control of the situation by barking orders at Klinq.

Astrid stood by Klinq coldly as he chided, "Stay there! She will see you perfectly from that spot!"

Klinq didn't know what the hell was going on. His mind was an odyssey, a blank world all of a sudden. It was crazy. He was standing in his cold spot, waiting for Contessia to see him and he had no inclination as to why. He didn't even know if Contessia would want to see him. Was this some ghastly plot cooked up by Isra, Astrid, and Contessia?

Astrid answered his question promptly as he perfectly positioned Contessia against the wall. Klinq watched horrified as Astrid reached for heavy iron chains behind her. They were quickly fastened around

133

both of her arms, much to Klinq's horror. Contessia didn't even realize what had happened until it was too late and she was chained up, unable to escape her fate.

She cried out, tears falling down her face as she asked, "Why are you chaining me here? What did I do?"

Astrid didn't answer her. He resented her crying. "Stop that! I've had enough of you to last a lifetime! Now be quiet!" he commanded as Klinq looked on.

Klinq was both heartbroken and angry. "Leave her alone! Let her go!" he shouted but Astrid ignored the gnome's frustration and proceeded to chain up Contessia's legs. She was chained to the wall in a standing position. She wasn't going anywhere!

Lady Isra had remained silent for the entire duration. It wasn't clear why she had been so tight lipped. She had left the room before Contessia had been chained up. It was so clear to Klinq that this whole debacle had been staged and planned to the very last immaculate detail!

Lady Isra returned an hour later. Her cloak dragged behind her as she ventured into the dim basement. She stood before Contessia and smiled weakly, knowing that the truth of the matter would be hard for the Wiccan girl to take. She had taken it upon herself to address the very frightened and confused Contessia. The girl had been kept in the dark long enough. Isra thought it was time to give her some peace!

Isra bent down before Contessia and placed her finger under the girl's chin somberly. "My dear child, this wasn't easy for me," she began as Contessia glanced at the witch with vulnerable eyes deeply filled with tears of hurt and betrayal.

"I don't understand!" Contessia whispered, a tear appearing boldly beneath her eye.

Lady Isra took Contessia's hand in hers and took a deep breath. She gulped. "I have to be bold with you, child. I found out you were under a spell from my nemesis, Everilda, and I needed to both guarantee her failure and your safety."

"All right," Contessia answered, doing her utmost to understand things from Isra's perspective, although her first impression was that Isra was indeed evil. Contessia wanted to believe that Isra did have good intentions that hid underneath her dark facade.

Contessia stared at Isra with disbelief as Isra continued explaining her reasoning. "I pondered this dilemma greatly before anything was decided. I did what needed to be done. I am keeping you here until I defeat Everilda! After she is gone, you will be free to roam as you please but you can never vacate this tower."

Contessia didn't understand those last few words. She was trying to process them in her mind. All she could clearly distinguish was that she could never leave the tower.

It was then that Lady Isra explained Contessia's fate. "I own your soul, child. You will stay with me until your last feeble days, but you will be protected."

Contessia stood staring at Isra, trying to take it all in. She was being protected, but Lady Isra owned her soul!

How Is this a good thing, she thought, *surely it can't be?* She was rife with skepticism. She wanted to believe there were good intentions in what Lady Isra did but all she could think was, *What will happen to me now?*

And she was right to think that because now that Lady Isra had full control over Contessia's soul, it wasn't clear just what her next move would be! Contessia had every inclination to be worried, that was for sure!

Isra noted that Klinq sat solemnly on the floor. She laughed to herself, as she had actually forgotten he was there. Klinq, however, had not forgotten. He sat cross legged on the floor with his head down, listening. He had listened to every word that had been uttered from Lady Isra's lips. He knew what he believed to be somewhat of the story now. He said somewhat because when it came to Lady Isra, there was always more than what it seemed to be! He had a sinking feeling that there would be more to this than what Isra had disclosed.

Klinq suddenly realized the witch had her eyes on him. He looked up as Isra addressed him.

"As eyes have deceived me, I finally set sight on my betrayer! I didn't bet my worth that you would be in cahoots with Everilda, but it is no matter now!" she retorted grimly.

He felt the delicious venom in her voice as the words were spoken. Klinq bent his head further, feeling the shame. He soon realized this act was stupid as she would reprimand him further for doing so, so he stopped. He stood upright to face her, his head slowly meeting her at eye level. It would take a very courageous man to face Lady Isra in such a heated conference of betrayal. Alas, much to his peril, Klinq was neither courageous, nor a man.

"I am sorry..." Klinq began. It was hard for him to admit that but as soon as he did, he felt a sense of relief. The relief was short lived, though!

Isra was not impressed by his admittance in the slightest. She thought of it as insulting to her glorious virtue, but she let him know just how insulted she was.

"Sorry is a far too precarious word in these times. It is spread around like butter!" she exclaimed as she folded her arms. She was cross with him, that was absolute!

Klinq relented, bowing his head in shame. "Forgive me, my mistress, but as soon as I got word that Contessia was caught up in this evil plan, I marched right up to Mistress Everilda and begged her to leave Contessia out of it!"

Isra noted his words and the way he was saying them and she nodded at him imperatively. "Very well. I can see you have nobility in your words. However, this matter still stands between myself and Everilda," Isra finished calmly. "In any case. You are no longer required in this establishment, Sir Klinq! "

Isra didn't give him a single second to utter his response as she turned to Contessia and immediately delivered her fatal message. "Contessia, I am sorry you had to learn it this cruel and disheartening way, but I couldn't let you linger in the deception any longer!"

Klinq stared at Isra and then glanced at Contessia in disbelief. He was flabbergasted. What on earth was she referring to? He scratched his head.

Contessia was bewildered after Isra had uttered these words. She too was thinking. Her thoughts were more aligned with Isra's but magic had a strong role to play in this. Naturally, now that Isra owned Contessia's soul, magic would now be a feature in all things!

Contessia thought soberly, *He has really done the dastardly thing to me! I can never trust him again!* She addressed Isra formally and questioned, "What has he done to me now?"

Klinq's face dropped figuratively to the floor. He couldn't believe that she could believe the words of Lady Isra, words that had been creatively instructed to demolish him in her eyes. Whichever way he looked at it, he was damned by her now!

Isra smiled. She snapped her fingers at once. The sound they made as her fingers touched echoed throughout the tower as her spell found its destination, shifting everything in sight into complete cataclysm. Isra snapped her fingers again, this time closing her eyes. A wave of icy blue cascaded over Klinq and Contessia. She admired her work for a moment and then shifted her attention to her original spell.

She waited as the shaking became more unrelenting. The entire tower felt her spell's wrath as it summoned its recipient. That recipient magically materialized in the basement much to Isra's glee. She rubbed her hands together triumphantly as the recipient stared blindly at her!

Cora, the cottage girl, was now in Lady Isra's fortress! She pinched the skin on her arms vigorously, hoping this was a dream. No such luck had befallen Cora on this day. She had been summoned by Lady Isra. And more devastatingly, this was no dream. It was indeed her reality!

She glowered at the scenery that unfolded before her: a cold, dank and grim basement. A girl chained up and even worse. Oh god, she stammered in her unconscious thoughts! The notoriously evil witch! Lady Isra of the dark!

"What the hell am I doing here? Why did you summon me?" Cora demanded.

Lady Isra hushed her, waving her finger at the girl. "Hush child, you should know better than to speak impolitely toward me! But to answer your question, do you remember our deal?" she questioned.

Cora got to work immediately. In her mind, images came to her unmercifully. She realized as the thought came to her. Cora stared at Contessia wildly. The guilt rapidly set in. She knew then that this was the girl whose soul she had helped Isra gain control of.

"Yes, I remember it. What of it?" she answered plainly.

"I need you to do one more thing for me," Isra responded.

"I'm not doing any more bargaining with you," Cora remarked coldly.

"Come now, child. You know you have no power over me! Why, if you don't do what I ask, I will simply kill your beloved father!" Lady Isra laughed. "He is in exile somewhere, is he not?" she added as Cora looked on.

Cora, noting the evil look on Isra's face, knew instinctively there was no getting out of this and glanced at Isra coldly, unhappy at being summoned to do the witch's bidding. And now even more so at Isra threatening her father. There was so much resentment in her eyes. So much resentment directed at the witch in this heavy moment.

She'd have killed Isra if she could. However, with Cora being mortal and Isra not, that would be a very tricky task. Cora simply relented, giving in to the vile witch's demands.

"Fine. What is it you want?" she said finally.

Isra laughed and replied, "I thought you'd never ask. Come with me!" Isra waved her finger at Cora, instructing her to come away with her.

Cora did as she was told. She followed the witch out of the basement to wherever it was she was leading her to. Klinq and Contessia were left blank as to what was going on. Literally. Isra had cast a freezing spell upon them both just before Cora had appeared. They would not remember a single thing. They stood in their motionless stances, frozen in time. Contessia's shocked but explicating face clashed wildly with Klinq's unspeakable sense of doom.

Cora meanwhile sat on Isra's couch, feeling a deep sense of

perplexity. A raven placed itself next to her, but she paid it no mind. Isra handed her a fresh cup of hot, steaming tea which Cora accepted despite the dark place she was in. Isra positioned herself in the seat next to Cora as she pondered their next transaction.

Isra didn't really like Cora. To be quite plain, she found the girl irritating. Just an annoying irritant that life bestows upon the world, that was how Isra viewed Cora. But in this delicate situation, the cottage girl had become useful. Isra had never forgotten the first occasion in which she and Cora had made acquaintance. Neither had she forgotten the debt that Cora owed her. If Cora thought that helping Isra gain control of Contessia's soul was meaning that they were done, she should think again!

Isra kept her eyes on the girl as she sipped her tea cautiously. It was a continuous battle of wits followed by fiery eye movement between the two women until Isra broke the ice.

She uttered, "I know you don't enjoy this or me. You have no reason to, but after we are done here, you can leave. You can go back to your merry life with the security that you will never lay eyes on me again. "

Cora took a deep breath as she prepared for the next outburst. She watched Isra's lips quizzically, wondering what would come out of those skin-covered contraptions.

"I brought you here for one reason and one only! I need you to cast a spell upon Contessia, yes the young lady you saw chained. The one we carelessly stole the soul from. In any matter, I need you to creatively engineer a fantasy for her to believe in, but it must be real. She needs to believe it is indeed the reality of things," Isra commanded sternly.

Cora processed this information carefully. A fantasy. All right! But a fantasy about what, exactly? This she did not have any knowledge of. Yet.

Cora smiled briefly and announced, "Okay, what kind of a fantasy? What alternative reality does she need to believe in?"

Isra reciprocated Cora's smile by exchanging a sly yet sweet one in her direction before replying. "She needs to believe that the one she loves, the gnome, has betrayed her!"

Cora exchanged figurative glances toward the witch. Okay, now this was insanely evil! How could she even contemplate such a thing? How unbelievably cruel! What a terribly unkind thing to do! Of course, she had no choice but to deliver this poor girl, her torturous fate.

Cora paused as she realized her thoughts weren't just for her alone. She then admitted, "All right, we can do this. I believe I know what needs to be done." She paused again, taking focus on Isra personally as she added, "Do you have a room I can work in?"

Isra chuckled cheerily. "Yes, you may use Contessia's old bedroom. It is vacant at present."

Cora acknowledged Isra and then added, "I will need some key ingredients to conjure this reality you seek for her."

Isra closed her eyes while smiling at Cora. In a flash, she was done with her task. "It is no matter, dear. Everything you require is now up there. Would you like any assistance?" Isra inquired thoughtfully.

Cora looked back for a second. Her face was plain and despondent. She then responded, "No, thank you. I'd like to get on with this and without you there. There will be fewer distractions."

Isra lounged around for what seemed like hours as she waited. Cora had been chanting and something was indeed brewing up there. Isra could smell herbs although she wasn't sure which kind. She lay down across her couch, her face motionless as she stared incoherently at the ornate ceiling. Her thoughts were busy and unfocused. Many images rushed around the intricate depths of her mind.

She caught sight of a raven, but she knew it was not Astrid. It was different, although like him, it was more charismatic in nature. This raven had strengths that went beyond power and knowledge of the occult. This raven focused on his emotions; that was its strength.

Isra gave this image nonsensical thought for a time, imagining that she was out in this wilderness, up close with this raven. Able to feel the softness of its feathers. Gently sliding her finger underneath his chin. She was in another world. She could see, feel, and touch every inch of this visionary image, and she knew at one point or another, she had been there! It was a wonderfully beautiful world.

This world was insolently stolen from her grasp as she awakened to find Cora staring at her, slightly amused that she had caught Lady Isra in a transfixion.

23

Isra composed herself right away. She lifted herself from the couch and turned to face Cora. She wasn't particularly amused by the snide smile that had materialized onto Cora's face. Nevertheless, Isra shrugged it off as she sat up, smoothing the wrinkles out of her long lace gown.

Cora was still smiling so Isra threw her an icy, cold look as she got to her feet. "Well, I hope by the smile on your face that the work is complete!" She folded her arms, appalled by the amusement on Cora's face.

Cora smiled again, which continued to infuriate Isra as did her unfathomable, cheery exterior despite where she was and whose presence she was graced with.

"Oh yes, everything is complete. She will believe that he has done all that we made her believe in!" Cora replied, still smiling.

Isra was getting more irritated and annoyed by Cora as the seconds passed. Both women faced each other in awkward, somber silence. Isra's mind began to wander needlessly into an illicit fantasy.

Isra imagined crushing Cora's skull on the sideboard with her fist. She began manically laughing as the blood pooled down the back of Cora's head, then slowly flowed into the base of Cora's neck. The blood illuminated everything as it waded into the material of Cora's dress. Isra felt remedied and satisfied that this irritating pustule of snot was destroyed. She realized Cora was still in front of her and suddenly engineered a much more cruel idea.

Cora turned to leave. "I guess this means our business is complete. Do not contact me again, Lady Isra of the Dark!" She turned her back to the witch.

"Not so fast!" Isra shouted. "I have a parting gift for you, child!"

Cora turned around with avid curiosity to face the witch.

With this, Isra twisted her hand around and with it came the most pulsating energy surrounding Cora and her entire being. It began to surround the poor girl and within seconds, black shards of glass began cascading down her spine, manifesting dark cords around the center of her heart that tugged at the core of her soul. Malevolent in nature. These cords held Cora down cruelly as the magic continued to whiz and swirl around its target.

Cora shrieked and wailed as the black energy surrounding her began to shrink her down in size. With every minute, it grew more unmerciful and showed her no sympathy as she was brought down to size. She was now in miniature form, small enough to fit in Lady Isra's hand.

How sweet, Isra thought as she admired her magical souvenir.

A glass jar appeared in Lady Isra's hand. Smiling merrily, she unscrewed its lid, malignantly swooping over Cora with the other hand, and then retrieved Cora and deposited her into the jar as she did her utmost to wail and shriek. Isra paid her no attention as Cora banged on the jar helplessly in her tiny state. She replaced the lid on top of the jar and screwed it shut, sealing it tight.

She began to recite a pleasing rhyme as she whispered to the victim occupant in the jar. "Oh sweet, pitiful Cora. Goodnight, sleep tight! Let's hope those torrid nightmares don't bite too hard! And now you are encased with jet black shards. They will not let down their guard!"

Astrid appeared around the door. He had been watching his love perform this act with a founding sense of intrigue. He made no haste as he called out, "Is that what I believe it to be? It seems so cute and not at all pretty!"

Isra placed the jar on the windowsill with a cackle and smiled. "All you need to know is it will never be you!" she responded ardently.

"Good to know!" The raven-man finished eagerly. "I never know just what you are cooking up in here! I do believe there is one problem left, although I could be wrong. Am I wrong?" he joked cheerily.

"Everilda!" Isra countered, acknowledging him fruitfully.

Astrid focused his attention on Isra as he placed his fingers beside her heart. "I think it is time she paid her ultimate price!" he uttered assertively as he delicately stroked around the nape of her neck, massaging the exterior and interior tension away. She, who was rapturously locked in his embrace as the day embraced the shadows that blithely became the night.

"I agree," Isra nodded sternly. "And her time will indeed come." She pulled away from him and turned to leave.

Astrid looked at her bewildered. She seemed so secretive. He thought, *Surely at this crucial moment, she would want me there? She would let me in!*

He waited for a while but she had not come back down to the lounge. Astrid eventually found Isra in their bedroom, standing in front of a grand mirror. He kept quiet as he enjoyed the view from his sacred spot.

He secretly watched her as she stood in front of the grand mirror in a glistening white dress, beautifully designed with white sequins that shone like crescent moons all the way down to the bottom of the gown. She admired herself as she turned around in the ensemble, loving how the material flowed so delicately on her slim frame.

Astrid couldn't help himself in this desirable moment. He snuck up behind her, placing his arms around her beaded gowned waist and kissed her neck, whispering, "You look beautiful, my love. Fit to be a queen!"

She gasped as she felt his energy pulsating all over her. Before placing her hand on top of his as she joked, "Oh, this old thing? It's been in my closet as long as I can remember! I do like the sweet sentiment."

Isra paused as she looked in the mirror for one last time, reminiscing, because this was to be her wedding gown. Now she would be wearing it to battle, right to the death.

24

Isra began to make haste as she made her way into the center of the forest, the old hideaway where Everilda dwelled. She had said her goodbyes to Astrid a few minutes ago. Although he had wanted to go along with her, he had understood that this was her battle and hers alone!

Isra's thoughts were dynamic, focused on war and completion. She knew that Everilda was going to fail, although a part of Isra had always known that. Everilda was far too obsessed with herself and her material gains to be able to win. This was Isra's trump card and she was going to use it.

Midnight was drawing near. Isra decided that she needed to add a personal touch to things. She was going to do what any resourceful and intelligent witch would do: she would summon Everilda and confront her herself!

Isra stood close to the earth, feeling the vibrations coming from underneath her. This was sacred ground or had been many moons ago. She closed her eyes, visualizing vibrant red in her mind's eye. It was vivid, like a flame. She enlarged it. Silently concentrating until it materialized into the night sky.

She shuddered with chills as the energy grew more potent. The red energy began to shoot off sparks of lightning. A gigantic shard of red lightning destructively attacked the sky, emitting its vile magic into the universe.

Isra stood back to admire her best work and then it began. The red lightning ferociously struck across the sky. It grew louder with every strike. It began to shift in a circular formation. The red energy sparks started spinning, swiftly spinning and twisting, violently turning until its work was done and in the midst of the forest Everilda stood.

She didn't look happy at being summoned. She pawed at her black and red cloak as red energy sparks attacked it during her journey here. She was fuming when her eyes laid sight on Isra's face. The vengeful mortal was not a happy bunny at all!

"Oh, I should have known it was you!" she muttered with a fiery temper.

"Long time no see, Everilda!" Isra barked.

"Why have you brought me here? Here of all places!" she demanded, stamping her foot needlessly, trying to make a big show, although Isra wasn't playing that game.

Isra made a snide chuckle at her nemesis. "You know, you of all people should know. I don't like to have things unfinished! You and I will be finished by the end of tonight," Isra chided with confidence, arousing Everilda's suspicions.

"How do you believe that to be so?" Everilda interrogated.

Isra had truly got Everilda's attention now. She wanted to know more. She wanted to know why Lady Isra of the Dark had summoned her here, motivated by personal reasons, when all these years Isra hadn't even acknowledged Everilda's measly existence.

Isra straightened her stance and stared at Everilda intensely as she thought a multitude of thoughts. She thought about Astrid and felt his presence, even though he wasn't here with her at this time. She needed to be clear on her mindset so she gave those thoughts extra mind allowing them to expand beyond her being.

She maintained her composure, laughing as she spoke to her old foe. "My dear, you may know many things, but I know one thing you don't have the knowledge of."

Everilda wasn't fazed and simply questioned, "And what is that?"

Isra smiled and it was her biggest, proudest smile you could ever imagine! She thought of Astrid again, this time closing her eyes. She thought of him and the love, beauty and magic they shared together as one. She thought of their strengths, their weaknesses and even their downtimes throughout their union.

As she continued to think these beautiful thoughts, a powerful surge went through her, emerging at the center of her heart, creating an energy of strong magnitude. An energy full of passion, love and caring. An energy so precious and red. It glittered brilliantly as her heart glowed with embers of love. It was not known for sure what she was feeling but it continued to grow and prosper, significantly becoming more powerful by the second.

It had been occurring for so long that she had forgotten about Everilda but it didn't matter. Isra and Astrid's love combined had materialized physically at the core of Isra's heart. It was physical and real. The energy was flowing all around the scene.

Everilda didn't really know what to do or say but she knew deep powerful magics were indeed at work. Her face dropped as she thought, *Oh shit, I'm done for!* What could she really say? She was no match for this energy. There was nothing she could do to stop it.

It continued to grow and now the red energy bursting from Isra's heart was expanding and surrounding the entire area between Isra and Everilda. It was only inches away from Everilda. Isra kept her focus on the energy, her eyes staying shut as it enveloped every aspect of her metaphysical being.

The red energy maneuvered to Everilda and started to attack her with a vibrant course of fiery sparks. It was at this moment that Isra opened her eyes. Isra looked at Everilda, now being covered with the fiery energy and smiled. Everilda looked at Isra weakly as it intensified and she was saturated in the redness.

Isra, still looking at Everilda, fixed her eyes to the sky and as she did so, she shouted as loud as she could for all to hear. "LOVE!"

It was this that was really magic. The word, "LOVE" was the undoing of Everilda because after Isra uttered that fatal word, Everilda was gone. All that was left was a pile of red dust. Everilda had been vanquished once and for all!

Isra smiled again, feeling overjoyed with her triumph. She was just about to celebrate her victory when a loud thunderclap shook the world and her along with it. She became unsteady on her feet. She tried to hold onto a nearby tree but to no avail.

The thunderclap grew louder. Isra looked up as the sound precipitated above her. She saw with her own two eyes a deluge of ice and snow, a deluge that was heading straight for her! She was its target! Within moments, the entire forest was coated in ice. Isra was in the thick of it all. Snowflakes gently covered all of her.

She laid herself down on the cold snowy ground, letting her head fall back as she concentrated, closing her eyes and picturing Astrid.

"Astrid, Astrid, Astrid!" she called out.

The snow vastly washed out everything as she lay in the center of the forest in the midst of bleakness and shimmery snow.

Back in the tower, Astrid suddenly had a thought. He didn't understand it, but it was clear and vivid. Lady Isra was laid on the icy ground, close to death. He didn't need any clarifications. He knew he needed to go to her now.

The snow showed no signs of stopping. Another loud thunderclap erupted in the dark sky. The snow gathered speed and spectrum, vastly becoming a catastrophic avalanche. The avalanche gained its strength and deadly power as it swept over the forest, clashing uncontrollably with the snow.

It was at this peak that the avalanche heightened, freezing over everything that nature had given to the forest. Its attention was focused on an enormous tree. The tree was covered in ice, but unable to contain the great weight of ice that had forced itself upon it. It began to shake and with it came icy shards as the tree lost its fight against nature.

Isra watched what was happening around her. She saw the shards of ice that were cascading and hitting everything. She looked up and saw the snow still in a white flurry, falling softly as it hit the earth.

It was with this that she saw large shards launching at heightened speeds straight toward her! She watched with horror as the shards raced to her body. A few seconds later, the shards, three of them to be exact, penetrated deep inside her stomach. Three of them stabbed her body, intently forming a triangle. There she lay, still conscious with the shards of ice deep inside her body. Blood slowly left the large slits they had formed inside her.

Still awake and still conscious, she caught sight of a figure beside her as she began to fade. It was Astrid. He had flown here in his raven guise as quickly as he could. It was inevitably too late. He looked at her helpless body as he whispered to her, "Not yet, please not yet."

Isra's sense of reality was fading. Her eyes grew heavy with the weight of the shards inside her stomach. Her eyes began to close with anticipation. Her world was barely in existence with the ebb and flow of her life force.

Astrid looked at her with his human face. He saw ravens all around Isra, gathering in their numbers. He examined the poignant scene before them as ravens swooped in from the trees and overhead beyond the lands and landed soberly beside Lady Isra of the Dark.

As the minutes passed, the witch who lay dying, fading into nothing, was surrounded and guarded by a sea of black ravens. Astrid had never seen anything like it before in his lifetime. He began to cry as the love of his life faded away in front of him. Isra's eyes were now closed. The forest was silent, in a catatonic state of mourning.

Astrid waved his fingers somberly and he was back as a raven. He didn't want to be a human any more. He had no need for the human body that Isra had given him. Without her, he had no need for anything. He was lost. Broken and in pieces. Wondering how he would face life without her.

Minutes passed, swiftly turning into hours. The night gently transformed into day. All that could be seen on the snowy graveside was a raven beside Lady Isra, refusing to leave her place as she eternally slept on peacefully. A jet black rose was placed on her heart by Astrid, held delicately by her cold, fragile hands.

Ravens all across the land had journeyed to the forest and gathered in their hundreds paying their respects. There they had flown in to watch Astrid mourning the death of his love. It was a very somber and poignant sight.

The sun ushered in a new day filled with hope and light. Light shimmered over everything, melting the ice and the snow faded away. It was after a time that Lady Isra's body disappeared from sight, a complete mystery as the raven Astrid had also vanished from that fatal, final spot. The spot of her victory and also her death?

Now that Lady Isra of the dark was no more, would Astrid take her place? Could there really be such a place where she was gone forever, never to grace the lands with her wickedness ever again?!

The End.

INTRODUCING HER DARK ROSE

DARK SPELL SERIES BOOK 7

Many believe death to be the end. But what if death is only the beginning of something else?

I'll have to elaborate on my meaning. We must go back to a time long ago, a time when a witch reigned supreme. She was both good and evil. Yes, she was both. She had no qualms about being both. She loved the darkness of the night. She admired the beauty in the twinkling stars. She also loved the light and brilliance of the sun.

It was black as night. A tall tower looked radiant in the distance, like a mountain that stood alone amongst the rest of the world. A white figure could only just be seen looking out of a window. She was dressed in white. She was a vision. When you looked closer, you could see her long white hair with delectable curls that framed her face and danced down her back. Her dress was torn, with three harsh slashes across her stomach.

This figure was Lady Isra.

She hadn't been seen for many moons. Many thought her to be perished. Even her lover Astrid believed she was no more. He grieved, mourning her tragic passing. It was a beautiful and somber scene with ravens all across the land gathering in their hundreds, coming together in a poignant moment to pay respects to Lady Isra of the Dark.

However, here she was, standing by the window. Alive and well in the ensemble that she had supposedly perished in. The tears across her dress marked the event, as did the scars on her skin where the ice blades had sank deep into her flesh.

So what had happened? Did she die? Or was she saved from some unrecognizable force? Whatever it was, it was evident Astrid knew.

The question remained as hours after her alleged death, Isra was able to breathe and Astrid gasped as her life force magically returned. Only one question stood still in his mind. Was she still immortal after this?

He feared she could be killed and that an attempt on her life would be made again. He had gone away on a quest to find an answer. He wanted to know for sure if Lady Isra was immortal as she had always been, or if she was now mortal. Her restoration wasn't that important to him, but finding out whether something like this would occur again was a much more worthy cause.

Astrid had been away on this soulful quest for three painful months. Painful because he needed and missed Isra. He felt the pain deeply in his heart. It tugged at his heartstrings as each day passed without her. He so wanted to talk to her and converse but he also knew he had to be strong in his mind.

Being away from Isra would ensure that nothing disturbed his focus in this important task. He felt that if he was alone, he would think better ... although being away from his love was pure torture. He couldn't wait for the day when he found himself in her arms again. He relished her touch. Just wanting to hold her and not being able to was harsh on him. It cut him deeper than he could imagine.

DARK SPELL SERIES READING ORDER

1. Her Dark Love
2. Kissing Darkness
3. Seducing Darkness
4. Queen of Darkness
5. Her Dark Soul
6. Her Dark Heart
7. Her Dark Rose
8. Darkness Reborn

ABOUT THE AUTHOR

USA Today Best Seller Isra Sravenheart resides in the UK. She is an avid reader, particularly in the fantasy and paranormal genres, and very much into all things fairytale and dark in nature. She is also a witty wordsmith.

Isra is known for being obsessed with coffee and very particular towards cats of which she owns four of the buggers.

You can follow Isra through her blog, or any of these social media platforms:

ALSO BY ISRA SRAVENHEART

The Dark Spell Series: Books 1 through 8

Heart of Oz

Tainted Siren

The Divine Spiritual Truth: A Twinflame Romance